godbox

Failing to find a trained-for position as slippered panta-
loon and shiftless ne'er-do-well, Tim Earnshaw turned
his first dollar as Tinseltown's premier fish trainer. His
well-drilled shoals may be seen in *Jaws*, *The Deep* and
The Abyss, while his subtle aquarium work graces many
a living-room scene.

When the market for briny blockbusters dried up, he
patented an ingeniously unprofitable Lint Moistener
before founding the now notorious Central Stalker's
Agency, being personally retained by D-list celebs for
conspicuous restaurant-pestering and yard-lurking.

Reduced to writing for a living by litigation and cruel
circumstance, his name has become synonymous with
all that is nifty and swell in the literary line. This slim
volume of exquisite *pensées* will enrapture his growing
fan.

Tim Earnshaw divides his time.

By the same author

HELIUM

TIM EARNSHAW

godbox

VICTOR GOLLANCZ
LONDON

First published in Great Britain 1998
by Victor Gollancz
An imprint of the Cassell Group
Wellington House, 125 Strand, London WC2R OBB
A Gollancz Paperback Original

A catalogue record for this book is
available from the British Library.

ISBN 0 575 06617 2

Typeset by SetSystems Ltd, Saffron Walden, Essex
Printed and bound in Great Britain by
Guernsey Press Co Ltd,
Guernsey, Channel Islands

98 99   5 4 3 2 1

To David 'Wiz' Wheeler

Hello, old friend

With massive gratitude to Ruthie Capella,
Anne-Sylvie Cerne, Don Cunningham, Charles Dzienis,
Francis Greene, Boris Glick, Robyn Kashket, Joel Peterson,
Gary Styling, Jim Thompson and Kathleen Tibbett.
I pinch your claws.

ONE

Beltway Bottom-Feeders

Cadogan Penn's table at Le Park was outside, behind a fern, practically falling over the white plastic chain onto the Sunset Plaza sidewalk, and had only slightly more cachet than a Safeway cart full of damp rags. The heavy coin was inside, being air-conditioned, and out here you were more likely to catch airplane waste than a waiter's eye.

Penn positioned his cellphone at a dynamic angle and poured a glass of the imported water that Steven had brought him instead of embarrassing him with the menu. He'd only gotten this table because Steven was a client of his, a guy who did a creditable Bruce Willis smirk while he waited on you between his acting career. Le Park was hardly A-list, but Penn wasn't there for Cher. This was strictly business. Today's dollar to collar: Dean Mance.

Penn turned the bottle so people could check the brand. Four bucks the bottle, he should get some return from his investment. Made out of icebergs from Finland or something. He shook a Monte Cristo butt from the cigar tube in his pocket and stuck it between his teeth. A crosseyed blonde at the next table shouted above the noise of the traffic.

—Hey! You with the cigar! Excuse me?

They didn't allow smoking at Le Park, not even outside, because it upset the delicate smog eco-system. In a town

9

where passive smoking held more vitamins than the air on the street, the policy made sense only to Hillary Clinton. Penn leaned back slightly so his head was over the chain, technically on the sidewalk, and lit the cigar with a tortoise-shell Dunhill.

—What? he said. What?

The blonde grimaced, craned her head around for a waiter. Lots of luck, thought Penn. He scowled at the traffic on Sunset Plaza, so close he could check his hair in the brightwork, and wished he had the trades with him to keep his hands busy. Dean Mance had told him you ate at Le Park to be *in* the trades, not read them. Hey, you want to read, go to a fucking library. Mance was about as heavy as they came at Le Park, a hyphenate with platinum lines to some real players, and a guy who got more ass than a sumo thong.

Penn was here today, farming melanomas, as he needed to grab some watercooler time with Mance about the new Nick Nolte. He was closeasthis to inking pact for his best-of-book, Tischia Burke White. Tischia was hotter than a car wreck, as he told Mance every chance he got. The proposed Girl By Pool credit would garner Penn an inside table at Le Park and concomitant high-end regalia. All she had to do was remember three words and fall into a pool. So naturally Penn was worried. Tischia Burke White was a girl who had to read her mantra off a wrist tattoo. And this falling business. It could go either way.

He sipped his water, keeping an eye out for Mance over his Porsche-design sunglasses. Lent a Cary Grant vibe, he liked to think. He was relieved when his phone beeped, and fought the impulse to grab it up right away like a schnook with nothing else to do. He let it sit there and beep a couple more times, thumbed the button, swung it up to his ear, checking covertly to see if he was being watched. He wasn't. The whole place was shrill with cell beeps, like exotic caged birds in the foliage.

—Cadogan, it's your mother, said his mother.

Momentarily fazed, Penn finessed it up. Aaron! he said loudly.

—Hello? This is your *mother*, Cadogan.

—Just fabulous! So, how was Paris?

—Paris? Is that you? This is your mo . . .

Penn lowered his voice to a whisper, maintaining the broad outdoorsy grin that teamed with the sunglasses, like in the ads.

—Mother, I'm at Le Park? No-one fields calls from their mother at Le Park, not even the baby Jesus, for crissakes.

—Cadogan, I think you may have forgotten, so I'm calling to tell you it's Arthur's birthday today, and I'd appreciate it if you would talk with him.

Penn slumped. Arthur Sloan III, aka Snakeboy, was his half-assed half-brother by his mother's second marriage, and a real drain on goodwill. The thought that he had crawled from the foot bath of his own gene pool always made Penn shudder.

—*Talk* with him? Okay, he sighed. Put him on, I guess.

—He's not here, Cadogan, I mean go to his place?

—He has a *place*? Great. I'll fax him.

—Cadogan, we have a problem. He won't listen, he simply will not listen. He's gotten beyond our capability to communicate with. He is just behaving totally inappropriately, and we believe there may be a drug situation. He looks up to you, and we feel in many ways, Art and I, that he needs the extended family at this time . . .

—He's twenty-blah years old, Mother, and he only looks

up to me when I step over him on the sidewalk. What can I do? Bond with him over a barbecue while he inhales the butane? Don't get me wrong. The extended family is a good thing. But does it have to extend in my direction? Hey, excuse me one second.

Penn had seen Dean Mance leaving the restaurant like he had somewhere to go, head down. Penn leaned back in his chair to give him a big hello. Mance didn't look at him and swung into his Porsche-design Porsche, valet-delivered to the curb. Penn called his name, Hey, Dean, breaking rule number one, never call out guys' names in restaurants, felt like a jerk as the Porsche slid away with its characteristic metallic motor flutter. He grabbed at the fern to keep him from lurching into a roller-blader and cursed silently.

—Okay, my meeting just got sidebarred. Thank you. So, tell me, what is this big trauma with Arthur, like he needs a brother all of a sudden as well as the hole in his head?

He heard his mother sigh. He could imagine her rubbing her eyes with the hand that held her sunglasses.

—Cadogan, please, try to talk some sense into him. He's just, dysphasic. He's really a sweet kid. He listens to you. Just be there for him. Be nice. Please?

It was Penn's turn to sigh. Okay, he said, he's my half-brother, I can be half-nice. Where exactly *is* his place these days? I don't think he's on my Rolodex.

His mother gave him directions, above an adult bookstore in Compton. I'll be carjacked, he thought. Even a pre-owned. He reluctantly agreed to go see the Snakeboy that pm in a window between taking meetings, and had his head in his hands when Steven came by. Penn moved the cigar under the table.

—I hope you're not recklessly abusing our no-smoking

policy, Steven said. We've had a complaint. Was the water excellent? May I squeeze you another?

—Steven, Penn said through a cloud of smoke, if you had a mandrill's ass for a half-brother and you had to *do* something with him on his birthday, without putting your rep in the toaster, what would you advise?

Steven drew his eyebrows together with forefinger and thumb and pursed his lips.

—That's good, said Penn appreciatively. Is it new?

—It's for Albee next week. Remember?

—He'll love it. Well?

—Oh, I don't know. Lapdancing?

Penn changed the subject and asked who Dean Mance was networking with.

—All Tinseltown heard you shouting his name. Have some *dignity*, Steven said, rolling his eyes despairingly.

—That's good too, said Penn. A *tad* camp, but hey. So?

—Couple guys from Fox, I think. Not my table.

Penn craned his head around and peered inside. Where? he asked, pointing a rolled five-dollar bill at Steven's stomach.

—Oh my, said Steven in a reverential whisper. We don't see many of *those* here. Brinks will bring your change.

—Any chance I get a table actually in the restaurant next time, or at least a fucking umbrella? I spent so much time on the sidewalk I think my teeth are tanning. I got smog sinus.

—They buy food, we let them sit in the restaurant. Crazy, I know, but it's policy. You want airconditioning, sit in your car. Or buy a cocktail, use the umbrella from that. They're at the center window to your left. They just got their check, I think. Be discreet, for god's sake. Bottom-feeders deplete the ambience of privilege we work so hard to engender.

Penn gave him a watch-it-buddy look while he checked his necktie, major-player full Windsor. Taking a last drag on the Monte Cristo, he carefully extinguished it on the edge of the table, stowed the butt. He walked purposefully inside like he had somewhere to go, exhaling a lungful of cigar smoke into the blonde's hair as he passed.

Le Park was a long room lit by a frosted green and blue glasshouse roof. Plants hung from the ceiling over cast-iron garden furniture. The floor was black and white diagonal checkerboard, with steps leading up to a kind of low mezzanine on either side, with tables behind a railing. A small raised stage at the far end with a green-painted baby grand which got opened at night, when they themed the place out for Hollywood tributes.

Penn had brought Tischia here a long time ago for the Pia Zadora Celebrity Roast. Back then she'd given him the impression she'd fulfilled her womanly destiny servicing his lower body parts. She'd undone the buttonfly of his chinos with her toes during appetizers, and by entrées the table had five legs. Those days, she'd have drunk a tub of his bath water. But that, as historians agree, was then.

He scoped the place out and saw the two suits up on the mezzanine. A waiter came up and asked if he had a reservation. Penn said thanks, his table was outside, he needed to talk to the gentlemen at the center table, nodded in their direction. He strode confidently up the steps and along to where the two suits were frowning at the check. One, the bulky guy, filling his slub silk suit like a diesel boat engine, working a toothpick. The other, small, bald, neat gray mustache, wearing a pale linen jacket and a silver necktie in a pattern of little fishes wearing top hats.

—Excuse me, gentlemen, Penn said. Have I missed Dean

Mance? He said to meet with him here. Cadogan Penn? He held his hand out to the big guy with the silk suit, who eventually looked up from the check, examined his toothpick and said, Who cares? Penn let his hand fall to his side. He didn't mention me? The suits looked at each other.

—Well, said the heavy, in a cigarette-torn voice, he did mention *that asshole* a few times. Could that be you?

The other guy chuckled. Don't mind my friend here, Mr, er . . .

—Penn. Cadogan. Cad.

—Sure. Usher. Edward. Ed.

Penn extended his hand and Usher gave it a brief third-person shake. The other guy, the diesel in the silk, slid a gold Amex across the table with a retina-puckering flash of finger jewelry accompanied by its own heavenly choir. A waiter swept the card up out of nowhere. Distracted, Penn hesitated a little in replying, breaking rule number two, never stammer at a suit.

—I'm representing Tischia Burke White? We're working with Dean on the new Nick Nolte.

The suits stood up, a waiter moving their chairs back for them, like it was making his week, he was so happy. Penn saw that Ed Usher wasn't small, it was the other guy who was built like two guys carrying a bowling bag.

—Whatever with *that*, said the big guy, rubbing his nose with a thumb the size of Penn's fist.

—Nice meeting you, grinned Ed Usher, and they left, parting a sea of swooning white-coated waiters ahead of them. Penn walked along the mezzanine muttering *Fuck you very much* under his breath, down the steps. In the mensroom he stole some wrapped soap from the metal lattice basket and a washcloth with Le Park monogrammed onto it, pushing

15

them into his hip pocket. He gazed absently at his reflection in the mirror, framed by a wooden trellis.

Ed Usher. Ed Usher. E.V. Usher. Nailed the guy. Used to be an independent, produced the *Vengeance* series back in the seventies. Retired but still associate producer for that daytime sudser *The Fires of the Heart, Hearts on Fire, Farts on Hire*, whatever. The big guy, Fox, Steven said. The fuck he knew.

Penn pushed his fingers through his hair, gave it a little loft. Caring-nineties boyish fringe pushed back from a tan forehead. Green-gray eyes, touch of manly blue shadow on a strong jawline. There was nothing *wrong* here. Except he was watching himself get poorer just standing there, and this wasn't a pretty sight. Everytime you see yourself, Mance had said, you want to be looking at a richer guy. If the slide continued he'd develop underachiever's slump, and people would flinch away like he was a human ear on a mouse's back. He splashed some house cologne onto his face and went back into the restaurant, passing Steven on his way back through to the kitchen.

—Any joy? smiled Steven, without waiting for an answer. Penn laughed mirthlessly, pretended to recognize someone off in the back of the room, clicking his fingers like a pistol. There was a bunch of 4Bs at the table by the door: baseball caps, beards, boots, beers. Tech crew he vaguely recognized, but all these guys looked alike.

—Hey, Cad, said one of them, raising his hand. They letting you use the restroom again?

Penn grinned and gave the guy a whitebread soul-grip.

—Hey hey. Good to see you. Who you working with, you can afford cutlery?

—Same crew. Just slumming down with the suits. You've met the guys? Guys, Cad Penn . . .

The guys smiled blankly at him. He nodded, paused, looked at his watch. Hey, look, I'm shedding sunlight. Let's spool up real soon, huh?

Out in the heat, he wondered at the iniquities of a business where a bunch of lens jockeys could eat inside at Le Park while he was sucking smog on the sidewalk, fielding calls from his mom. He went around the back and beeped his BMW open in the lot. Valet parking was harder to get than a *New Yorker* cartoon. A short Italian-looking guy walked up and presented him with a card.

—Hi. I'm Paul George, he said in a deep warm voice. If you need my look, call me. Thank you for your time, and enjoy your day.

Penn flicked the card out the window and headed south to the Santa Monica freeway, fender to fender with all the other creeping cellphone booths, fumbling up Tischia Burke White's number on memory. What I should have said, he thought to himself, was I was always a John Ringo man myself. That would have been very funny.

—Tish?

—Did you pick up the suit?

—Huh? Not as of now, hon, I'm helming a meeting. I'll pick it up later, I promise. Listen, I just did lunch with Ed Usher?

—Tonight just won't happen without that suit, it's like *really* important. I can't believe you haven't done this for me.

—*E.V.* Usher, right? The producer?

—My celebrity spot on the Shuggy show tonight is falling

at a real propitious time. My aromatherapist says the odors are good tonight. There's a hint of bougainvillea coming in from the mountains and that, as you know, is my keynote scent. My ensemble *has* to be in harmony with it. I'm in wardrobe at six, you know that . . .

—Jesus, Tish, listen, I can put you up for *Flames of the Heart*. A glide-by to get you established, build to a regular. You'll be sensational.

—It's the color. I'm creating my entire maquillage around it. Peach accents. What did you say?

—Huh?

—*Fires of the Heart*?

—I'm in bed with the producer. He loves me. We're going to . . .

—Isn't that daytime? Do I *do* daytime? I don't think so. Oh, here's my voice coach; I have to find my sides. The *suit*, Cad. Ciao for now.

Penn squeezed the phone in his fist and grunted at it like a hog through his clenched teeth until his pulse rate slowed to a waltz. Doesn't *do* daytime? What is this shit? One lousy pool fall in a Nick Nolte feature and she's not *doing* daytime? A voice coach? For three fucking words? Her aromatherapist? Excuse me? Who *were* these people?

He shook his head, wondered when he'd ever get his break in this town. For crowding a decade now he'd been hustling deals on the edges of the picture business, parachuting his father's legacy. A limo rental. A catering business. A public domain programming shop, selling bundles of grainy wildebeest documentaries and Canadian cartoons to no-budget cable stations. And H$_2$Ollywood, the gourmet water consultancy he'd created to supply bottled water on-set, wherever. Downloaded it to a couple of Greek brothers who strangely still thought they'd got a great deal, honked and waved every time they passed him in their Lincoln Town Car.

Then he'd sunk pretty well everything into setting up CPA. CPA for Cadogan Penn Associates, of which he was it. There it was on the buckslip he'd had printed up and clipped to his roster books. Nice logo in classic serifs, and, at the bottom, Cadogan Penn, CEO. He'd built up a small stable of minor but saleable talent; contacts he'd made driving cars, slinging hash and selling bottled icebergs. Poised for noise; his 'fiancé', Tischia Burke White. Who was now doing diva on him.

Penn had morphed so smoothly from lover and mentor into dumb gofer, he was whiplashed from getting up to speed on the situation. Fetch this, do that. She had this spot tonight on the Shuggy Kristiensen Show, primetime cable nuts-n'-sluts. Which he'd set up himself, as a result of getting the virtual certainty in the new Nick Nolte. Which he'd set up himself. And for what? For a living-room office so far off the Strip you had to put your watch back, a table in the fucking street at Le Park, and a pre-owned BMW sedan, which he told everyone had been given to him by Wayne Newton. This was almost true. He'd bought it from Wayne Newton's pool man. Good price, too. Not actually the pool man himself, of course, he drove a new de-badged SE with body-color skirting, but his assistant. The one who did the pec-flexing stuff with the big plastic hose, sucking up syringes and shit your houseguests leave you. Penn had fit personalized plates – CALL CAD – fabricated, as these things were, at Folsom Prison. The con thoughtfully included an ASS HOLE plate on his own initiative. Penn had considered starting up a pool service, but how did you get the clients? Knock on

19

people's doors with a big fucking brush? How great could that look?

Representing Tish had seemed not only an easy but a logical option. She'd built an impressive showreel of ad work; *Earl Corrigan's TireDrome*, the *BabyKlense* account, *Fresh-All-Nite Pantiliners*. Plus a spread in *TV Top*, followed by a celebrity leg-cross on *The Kathi Show*, and some tits-n'-teeth work on *Homicide Love*, straight to video, *but hey*.

All this plus the day-to-day pouty stuff that paid the bills. So her profile was cresting everywhere. A profile made that much more crestworthy by the dual silicone chest puppies Penn had bought her as an engagement gift. To protect her bridgework when she walks into walls. Touch of old-timey romance.

Now, if she could just manage to remember her line, *Hey, no problemo!* the piece of business with Nick Nolte could start to shake the dollar tree. But here she was, doing diva on him. It was a creepy feeling. And he knew she'd been fielding calls from her old agency, too.

He punched in a Kenny G cassette and cut south onto the 110, following his mother's directions, past the pylons and the billboards and the dusty lots with sullen hooded kids hanging out under the hoops, feeling Urban Fear Syndrome suck his stomach walls together. Unlike New York, where you can find yourself in deep shit in the space of an intersection, LA's jeopardy envelope is more frayed at the edges, and that much harder to get out of. Penn's knowledge of this area was pretty much restricted to helicopter news-reels, and that's how he liked it. The other side of his world.

He hit Tuscadero Street, with its Pacific Rim shoe marts, barricaded liquor stores and clawed dayglo posters, thinking this was where they kept all the *ugly* in the world. Buildings made of fiberboard suitcases smeared with cement, matt-finish cars with fender crimps. Penn had a savage jones for a tall latte, a fern in a window. Porn Baron (Mature Books 'n' Video's) was right under a ragged end of freeway offramp they'd quit building when they saw where it was going, just dropped their shovels and ran screaming into the hills.

Penn parked the beamer by a sawn-off meter, making a big production number of zapping the alarm with the remote, and stood on the sidewalk feeling queasy with apprehension. The distorted thump of music from behind the door with the nuclear-waste sticker was making it buzz visibly on its hinges. He could just get back in the car and make an excuse. That wouldn't get rid of the obligation, but spending two minutes with the guy would.

Penn nudged the door open with his toe, recoiling from the gust of noise and stink. He picked his way up the steps, negotiating the broken glass and greasy takeout husks, holding his breath against the saturated vomit odor. Steeling himself, he crossed the threshold into the fetid squalor of his half-brother's half-life.

The windows had been painted black, and the words CRASS, EXPLOTED, and UKSUBS crudely scratched out with a knife. In the light that cut through the letters Penn made out Snakeboy crouched over a mattress in the corner. There were Cherry Coke cans and, bafflingly, blister-packed Cuisinart accessories strewn everywhere. The shuddering cassette player was hotwired to the ceiling lamp.

—Arthur? he yelled. He could see the green spikes of Snakeboy's punk hair, and the white A-in-a-circle painted on the back of his leather jacket. He hadn't heard. Penn reached up and yanked the wire out. *Arthur!* In the sudden silence Snakeboy twisted around, pushed something under the mattress. His face was pallid, shiny, and tight with zits. A spiderweb tattoo covered one cheek.

—Fackin' *ell*, man, you *cant*, what the *fack* are you doing?

—Happy birthday, said Penn, going to the window and squinting out through the C of CRASS to check his wheels. Nice place you got here. Who's your stylist? Ted Bundy? Do these windows open?

Arthur wiped his nose noisily on the back of his hand.

—You could of given me a fackin' coronary, man. Birthday?

—I brought you a gift, Penn said breezily. He lobbed the Le Park courtesy soap and the washcloth onto the mattress.

—The fack's that? grunted Arthur suspiciously.

—Soap. You use it for washing?

—Oh, very fackin' amusing. You're a real comedian, Cadogan.

—Let's go for a drive, Arthur, get some fresh air. Or, hey, open a window.

—Why? And my name, said Arthur, prodding Penn in the chest with a rooty forefinger, is Snakeboy. Look. He dropped to the floor, knees like waxy chicken bones poking through the frayed holes in his tartan bondage pants, hunted through the debris, surfacing with a 45rpm vinyl record. The cover picture featured the swastikas on his butt cheeks.

—Nice, said Penn. This what you call yourselves, Niggers On Skis? Your mother must be so proud.

Arthur pointed to the hand-scrawled text beneath the picture. Lead vocals, Snakeboy. Not fackin' *Arthur*, right? Check it out.

Penn pointed to the window and frowned. Uksubs? What's that? And there's no such word as *exploted*. Can we open it or what? It's pretty damn skunky in here.

Arthur bared his nasty-looking teeth in a terrible marshy blast of laughter and halitosis. Then he got serious, fixing Penn with a flinty ratlike stare. Why're you here? he said. Whadya want?

—Stop fucking *poking* me, will you? said Penn, backing away. Your mother sent me, okay? I'm doing her a favor, as she's my mother too. She and your father are worried about you. Why, I don't know. Look how you look. Great decor, career, nice clothes and everything . . .

Pleased with the compliment, Arthur admired his slug-trailed leather jacket. S'English, man, quality tailoring.

—What is this English thing you've got, Arthur? Fackin' this, fackin' that . . . Didn't they teach you anything at school? It's *fucking* this, *fucking* that. The g is optional. Can we open . . . What's that?

Arthur crimped his spiderweb tattoo, listening to the sound from the street. *Fackin'* car alarm, man . . .

Penn was already halfway down the stairs, skittering on squeaky styrofoam. Out in the street, blimp-boy leaning in through the smashed side window of his beamer, working the radio loose. Hey! Penn shouted, dodging between the traffic. The fat guy turned round slowly, holding the Bosch cassette-radio. Like a lot of LA, he was dressed for a snowboard vacation; hooded Tommy Hilfiger sweatwear, NBA balloon shoes, knit cap, goatee beard, Killer Loops. What the fuck are you doing? yelled Penn over the skwee-skwee-skwee of the alarm.

—This your car? said the fat guy, inclining his head toward the BMW. Penn stopped in his tracks, no longer totally excited by the strength of his position.

—Huh? Yeah, it's my car . . .

The fat guy weighed the radio in his hands thoughtfully.

Well, he said reasonably, this will be your *radio* I'm stealing, motherfucker. What do you *think* I'm fucking doing?

—Fack off, nigger! Arthur added, unasked, over Penn's shoulder. The fat guy tilted his head, like he was hard of hearing.

—The fuck he say?

—Nothing, said Penn quickly. *Take* the stereo. Hey, you want the tapes? You like Streisand?

—Smack his fackin' head in, said Arthur, nudging Penn in the back. The fat guy took a step toward them, swinging an aluminum baseball bat that had appeared, mystically, from nowhere. Penn raised his hands. Hey! Really! Take the . . . *shit!* As the bat flashed in the sun, they turned and ran, Arthur tripping over the straps on his bondage pants. They skidded down an alley, vaulted a wino, ran down behind an auto shop, scattering a pile of mufflers, people yelling, vaulted a yard fence, down another alley.

—In here, grunted Arthur, diving through an open window. Penn swung a leg over the sill and fell in on top of him. They lay in silence for a while, Penn straining his face away from Arthur's head, which smelled like roadkill.

—I'm trying to think, he said weakly, how this could possibly be worse. Maybe if we had beards, or this was Germany. Arthur snickered, pushed out from under. Where are you going? said Penn, a note of rising panic in his voice.

—Check it out. S'no-one here, they'd of heard us, man. Stay here and watch for fat niggers with baseball bats.

—*Arthur!* Penn hissed furiously, but he was gone. His pinhead half-brother was going to turn over a stranger's apartment, and a guy the size of a cow was chasing them with a baseball bat. He thought back to when he could sit in the sun and sip icebergs at Le Park and almost wept with nostalgia. It all seemed so very long ago. He peeked out over the sill. No-one. He could hear Arthur going through the closets. *Arthur!* Get the fuck out of there!

There was a sound in the alley. Someone was coming. Big crunchy footfalls. Penn sank to the floor beneath the window, whimpering, biting his knuckles. The footsteps got closer, Penn heard whistling. Guy looking for a little baseball bat activity, would he whistle the theme from *Bewitched*? Whoever it was took like forever to disappear.

Penn opened his eyes and looked dully around the room. There were torn sixties-psychedelic-style posters tacked to the wall, a bunch of ratty old vinyl albums and an electric guitar on a busted-up couch. Some kid's idea of a hippie pad. With a jolt he noticed someone standing in the doorway. Took a second or two to recognize him.

Something about him was strange. *Majorly* strange. Not just the way he stood, although that was subtly different, but his face. It was open, sort of childlike. It had color in it. And it was smiling. A hesitant kind of smile, like it was waiting for approval or something. It looked like Arthur, yet not like him. More like the little kid Penn used to swing laughing into the couch. But more like a mature adult, too. Both younger and older at the same time. And when he spoke, in a voice with no trace of the Dick Van Dyke faux-cockney, his words were more shocking than any Penn had heard him use for a long time.

—I'm sorry, Cad.

Penn was stunned, silently mouthing the word *sorry*, face a shifting mask of confusion and bewilderment. Sorry? As in apology? Snakeboy? Something was not tracking here. As his half-brother came over, Penn watched the change in the very way he moved, held himself. Arthur hunkered down in front of him.

—Cad, this is not right for us to be here, he said, helping Penn to his feet. Let's go, huh? I tidied up back there. Are you okay? You look upset.

—Upset? said Penn, finding his voice. I'm not upset. We've just bust into some guy's apartment because the psychopath who trashed my car is chasing us with a baseball bat. Why should I be upset? I'm okay. Are you okay?

Arthur grinned. Everything's going to be fine. Don't worry.

On their way back to the street Penn kept stealing glances at this strange new person, trying to figure out what had happened. Arthur looked taller, too, maybe because he was walking different, lost the slacker slouch.

—Arthur, he said edgily, the guy may still be there, biting off the body panels . . .

—Don't worry. He's gone. I'm real sorry about your radio, I'll see what I can do. I think I know the guy from around.

He bent down and unclipped the bondage strap from his knees, rolled it up, put it in his pocket. That's better, he said, shaking his head. I was wondering why I couldn't walk.

—It's only a radio, said Penn. Not worth getting your spine hooked out on a tire iron for. Really.

Arthur smiled like his face was set naturally that way, not like it was an effort or fake or anything. And was it a trick of the light or was his tattoo fading? Had he been cleaning his teeth? What was going on?

—I really appreciate you coming out this way to see me, Cad.

26

Penn made a whaddyacrazy? face, realized that Arthur was being totally, simply, sincere. No problemo, he said. Hey, we're family.

Penn drove away leaving Arthur clearing up the broken window glass in the gutter. He ground his teeth thinking this through, rubbing his jaw, grimacing. Maybe the kid had seen sense all of a sudden, just took a few words from a respected elder brother to bring it home to him. Maybe the gift of the soap had awakened some dormant cleanliness gene.

Or maybe the guy was warped out of his hat on something he'd scarfed back at the hippie pad. But sweeping up the glass? Waving goodbye? Apologizing? *Cleaning up?* What kind of terrible, DNA-twisting drug made you *tidy*?

Or maybe, and Penn grew chill at the thought, his half-brother had been replaced by an alien life-form. Sinister emissary from an interplanetary tidiness force. He checked his wristwatch. Shit! The suit! A white-knuckle drive back across town found him beating his fists on the shutters of Larry N' Barry's Kleen-King, yelling, It's four-thirty! You're open! A window above the door slid up noisily and a guy wearing what looked like a woman's satin slip leaned out.

—You're right, honey, it's four-thirty, he said. You're wrong, they're closed. Now be nice and fuck out of here.

The window slammed shut. Penn gave the shutter a vicious kick and shouted up at the window. And peach is *not you*, asshole! He got back into the car. There were still crumbs of safety glass in the upholstery and they bit into his butt like baby Rottweiler teeth. He hit the redial button on the cellphone.

—Uhh . . .

—Unless I get that suit in like five *minutes*, Cad, I just don't know what I'm going to do, I really don't, I'm a mess of stress . . .

—I am trying to tell you, honey, he said evenly, that I'm at the drycleaner's and they have somehow misplaced your suit. It's not lost or anything, they just can't find it. I'm here over an hour. There's been a ticketing problem and they've sacked the girl responsible, on the spot, so that's indicative of how much weight *we* carry here, which is like a good thing, right? They've been going crazy trying to find it, they're really clear on how important it is to you, and how important you are to them. Everyone's really tense about this and there's been some crying. So my request is, you got other clothes, take another suit to the studio. Hang tough, baby, do the chant thing. We're really giving a hundred and ten on this. I love you, honey, you'll be wonderful, okay?

—It's not just the suit, Cad, she snuffled. It's like indicative of a whole attitude I've been picking up? Like you're just not giving me the commitment my career needs right now. And how am I getting to the studio? Everything's falling apart. And my aromatherapist says we must both be in a listening place for my upsetness . . .

—I'm in that place, sweets, I got a seat right at the front. Mellow it out. They told me they'll cab the suit to the studio, directly they locate it, at no charge. Okay? Hey, *no problemo*, huh?

—They have to locate the studio? This is terrible . . .

—It's okay, honey, I'm on my way. Bite a Prozac, read your mantra.

He pressed the *end* button and found himself spooling through the whole Tischia thing. They'd first met when she'd been hostessing a trade show where he'd supplied the limos. Thong bikini with a WonderWienie rosette on each breast, little tray of snacks, *fantastic* big mouth that reminded him of Carly Simon. Not all of Carly Simon, just her mouth. Kind of lips you could crawl through and fuck from the inside, curled up on the tongue. Outstanding, just totally.

Back then she'd been Tricia White, trying to break out of hooter movies on stroke TV, go legit. He'd given her a new name, a casaba boost, hustled her away from her agent, who'd placed her in dump-bin clunkers like *Thong of Norway*, and *E-Womanuelle III*. This same sack of sleaze who was now sending her flowers. So gentlemanly, and why didn't Penn think of little touches like that? Because he was too busy being cold-cocked in restaurants and counseling dysfunctional family members and picking up the goddam *laundry* to hang around fucking florists all day, mainly.

He had to cue up something else fast before his contract with Tish fell apart like Kleenex in the sink. This contract, drafted 'as a favor' by a friend who sold thermal roof sealant – whatever with *that* – had been constantly pattern-disruptive for Penn, more holes than a junkie's arm. Essentially, she was legally free to ankle at any time, taking his silicone with her. Whole deal hung by the skin of his teeth. Penn suspected she knew this, in spite of her dumb ickle-girlie act. He didn't trust her, and their engagement was now as loose as the contract.

He flamed up the Monte Cristo stub, trying to imagine he was a mountain stream tumbling through a pine forest like in that new-age book Tischia'd made him read.

—Fuck it, he said softly on the exhale, watching the gray smoke coil against the windshield. Fuck it and the box it came in.

TWO

Cuckoo Couch Confidential

The Shuggy Kristiensen Show went out live from a storefront studio on the Strip, between the Latimer Hotel kitchens and the Scientology store. Two cameras, one locked in close-up on Shuggy for reaction cutaways, the other for the two-wall set and lensing the lowlife on the sidewalk, pressing up against the window like diseased fish. Shuggy stole the concept from the old Dave Garroway show, but here the sleaze was the beef. Every show he'd feature a couple of guests off the street on the Cuckoo Couch. People with clinically damaged behavior patterns made for the kind of toe-curling viewing that had kept Shuggy in the business for thirty years, minus a few in the slammer sponsored by the IRS.

Before cable, before he even did TV, Shuggy'd been a radio jock back in the sixties, beaming out of K-LUB, a two-watt transmitter in the desert. He'd called himself Shuggy The K until Murray The K sent his lawyer over to put a foot on his neck. The unthinkable prospect of ante-ing up for representation moved him to pen a curt note of capitulation, and drop the K. But here he was, thirty years down the line, his own show, a real Hollywood survivor. Still used the same corny lines, wore the same Botany 500 box-cut jacket and signature white turtleneck, topped by the same hundred-mile-an-hour pompadour.

The Shuggy Show rated in the high twos, an attractive proposition to owners of Tire-Dromes and drive-thru taco franchises, but nowhere near enough to give the webs a hard-on. And tonight the formula was the same as ever. Ray people and a hooter girl. The guy who claimed to have seen his neighbor fly showed up incapable of retaining body waste and wasn't allowed through the door. An emergency back-up flake was plucked from the line of hopefuls on the sidewalk. He wore pan scourers taped into his undershorts, to counteract CIA sterility microwaves. Kind of entry-level for a ray person, but Shuggy cut him a deal. Change CIA to IRS and he was on the couch. The guy considered, said okay.

His couch buddy was a teenage baglady with food in her hair, and nipple rings wired to her pager. *Why* was kind of immaterial, as she'd promised to show some tit.

Under the lights the guy with the steel wool in his shorts developed a major sweat-gland problem, started to peel off his clothing and wring it out, to sounds of self-indulgent disgust from the crew and the crowd on the sidewalk. This kind of thing was not uncommon on Shuggy's show, and the camera stayed put just long enough to prevent an infraction. The bag-girl edged so far away from him, now naked and masturbating, she fell off the couch. Shuggy's doorman threw the guy out while Shuggy helped the girl back up on the couch, copping a nice feel and waggling his tongue for the camera. It transpired she'd engineered the whole thing to give her rock band a namecheck. Shuggy went along with this because she showed how the wires were attached, and he liked tit second only to old banknotes. Real money; dead presidents you could count out on a motel bed. That was the best thing in all the world, but tit was okay.

After the break, when the girl was hustled back out onto the street clutching her autographed I BEEN ON SHUGGY tee she'd been pleased to pay thirty bucks for, Tischia perched prettily on a leg-revealing barstool while Shuggy shook a fake cocktail at a retro-styled bar. She was a regular favorite from back when she'd fidgeted astride remolds for Earl Corrigan, moaning *If I were a car I'd want Earl Corrigan rubber on my rims.* The big joke being, even reading the line from the cue card, she kept getting it wrong, blushing uncontrollably when she said *rubbers.*

Tonight she was returning as a star, wearing a tight citrus bolero top, zebra vinyl cigarette pants, and red stilettos. She read some cute adlibs off the cue sheets held up by the cameraman, flashed that smile and leaned forward so her neckline gaped winningly. Shuggy asking her about Nick Nolte, was he as, you know, *big* as he looked on the screen. Tischia, cute and professionally discreet, successfully giving the impression that there was something to be discreet about, and apparently Demi Moore was no longer involved in the project which was like a real shame?

Penn sat back in the control room, where he could keep an eye on his car through the street security camera. Hey, he said to the young guy riding the faders. Anything wrong with that outfit she's got on? Strike you as anything less than fantastic?

The kid told camera two to roll back for a legshot, stared at the monitor. Why? he said.

Penn spoke through a cloud of cigar smoke. Ah, no reason, I guess. You heard her earlier, bawling me out in front of Shuggy.

The kid shook his head. I don't wanna be involved in that shit.

Penn looked at him. Twenty years old. Surf dude with his hat on backward. Big-time cable director. Excuse me? Penn said. You don't want to be involved? What is this shit? Jesus.

The kid told camera two to pan to the street, get some drool shots, while he stabbed up the sponsor's message. Then he turned to Penn and said, You wanna smoke, go sit in the street, okay?

After the show Shuggy took Tischia, and unavoidably Penn, to the Titanic, the new niterie off Melrose, where the food was European art statements poised tellingly against the post-modern deconstructed decor. Penn discovered he'd ordered something glistening and twitchy, like a Japanese endangered species fetus.

—Is this thing blinking at me or what? he said. He poked it nervously with a fork while Shuggy squeezed his arm around Tischia, making her cleavage surge, whispered some-thing in her ear. Tischia giggling and wriggling like she used to do with an Earl Corrigan remold stuck up her heinie.

When the check came Shuggy was inevitably schmoozing it up at a table the other side of the room. Penn snatched up the tab and signed for it so hard he broke his pen. Tish just loved it all, kissing her darling Shugster on the cheek out on the sidewalk, kids leering, Hey, Shuggy, give her one for me! Penn drove her home in silence while she checked through her maquillage case.

—What I don't get, Penn said eventually, is you writhe all over that fucking geriatric for five lousy minutes on cable, but you *don't do daytime*. You understand my confusion here.

Tischia continued to rummage in her makeup, and her reply was muffled by the brushes between her teeth. You fixed this up, Cad, remember? I did this to help him out, lend the show some class. Plus it's great PR to my fanbase. And it was gentlemanly of him to escort us to the Titanic.

—Escort is right, said Penn. See who picked up the tab? *Moi.* And he only escorted us there because Titanic begins with tit. *Gentlemanly*, my ass.

Tischia got everything stowed away to her satisfaction and ran the gilt zipper around the case top. You can be really gross, Cad, you know? And would you close your window? And that cigar is, you know, like, yucky-*pucky*.

—Oh, hey, *excuse* me. Knit a fucking forgiveness quilt with my name on.

They remained as silent as the cool breeze coming through the busted window, until Penn pulled up at her dinky house in Culver City. She just loved the old-timey vibe, and her aromatherapist had hung bundles of dead weeds on the porch.

—Goodnight, Cadogan. I'm real tired.

Penn drove home feeling tired, too. Tired of being told to sit in his car if he wanted airconditioning, in the street if he wanted to smoke. Tired of being the last link in the food chain. Tired of staring bottom-feeders in the ass. He unthinkingly stuffed a Curtis Stigers cassette into the gap left by the radio, cursed repeatedly, threw the cassette out the broken window.

—Cadogan? he said quietly, in a tone of baffled hurt. *Cadogan?*

THREE

Fly Threads

Next morning Penn dropped his car off at the BMW concession to get the glass fixed; no problem, they'd cannibalize a write-off in the shop. No point in buying new for a heap of shit like his, obviously. He got them to organize a rental as they said their courtesy cars were all out on the road. Sure, thought Penn, but they *wouldn't* be if he drove *this* year's model.

He hung around the lobby drinking decaff latte from a cardboard cup with a JavaJacket around it, wondering how in hell you got up the scratch for a BMW franchise, until the rental turned up. Subaru with a glandular paintjob, ideal for Hispanic hair artists on a budget. Oh, fabulous, said Penn to nobody in particular.

He drove by the photo lab to pick up Tischia's new set of contacts and, back at his apartment, spread them out on his desk, squinting at them through a little fold-out magnifying glass. She looked undeniably gorgeous, a natural natural. They'd done the session at the beach, like those Marilyn shots, full of sun and fun and silicone. One frame looked like she was being choked by her own breasts. Alarming. The phone rang.

—Cadogan, said his mother, this is your mother. I, we, Art and me, just can't thank you enough, I simply don't have the words.

He rubbed his eyes to get the room in focus and waited for his brain to follow through. Huh?

—*Arthur!* laughed his mother. Penn remembered the weird stuff with Snakeboy, stuff that had been really too strange to think about for too long as it made his brow knit up unattractively.

—Oh, he said, sure . . . no problem. Really, it was a pleasure. I guess.

His mother cut in, unable to contain her enthusiasm. And we want you to come visit with us for a celebratory family dinner, tonight.

—I think I have a window.

—See you here at eight. Thank you again!

He frowned, scratched his head, shrugged, called Tischia. Got her machine, Stevie Wonder singing 'Isn't She Lovely?'. Tish, he said, Cad. I just got the contacts from the beach shoot and you are sensational. Let's take a table in the am and finalize the book shots. I can't meet you tonight because I'm doing family, but call me anytime. Oh, I'm picking your suit up, they finally located it and they want to buy you some flowers or something. I really bawled them out on this one. Take a me pill, baby . . .

His mother lived with her second husband, Art Sloan II, in her cottage on a private estate east of Zuma Beach. You swung off the PCH and followed this sandy road past Tommy's Tiki Kabana, unlocked a corroded metal gate, drove until you saw a row of five clapboard and shingle cottages right there in the sand, built up on stilts to get a view of the ocean.

They'd been built in the forties by Columbia as retreat cottages for screenwriters, idea being to give sensitive types a bit of *space* to allow the creative genius to blossom. But they were too far from the studio, writers got sick of having to rush back to attend rewrite meetings every eleven minutes, finished up moving back to the flea-infested flophouse on the back lot.

Over the years the cottages had evolved into this kind of self-precious artistic community, with a strict code of occupant eligibility and behavior enforced by a fascistically liberal Columbia Cottage Committee, which Penn had on occasion spelled with Ks. He'd spent his summers here as a kid, before the cultural claustrophobia began to cramp him out.

Now the cottages were inhabited by a thriller writer who blew away Havana Club empties with a pump shotgun (this considered acceptably *outré* as long as he kept the choke closed, shot into his shielded sandbag wall, and observed the time restrictions); an Eastern European sculptor who did savagely uncompromising work with beach debris (Jane Fonda had attended one particularly memorable *vernissage*); a couple of very pleasant guys in interior decoration; a pet telepath; and Margaret 'Muffy' Penn with her disturbingly gynecological watercolors and her disturbingly anal husband. Muffy, as the only second-generation resident, headed up the Committee and chaired the monthly meetings held at Tommy's Tiki Kabana. They all felt terribly protective about Tommy's place, paradigm as it was of a California culture that needed their sensitive guardianship if it was to endure.

Art Sloan lectured part-time in Gender Studies at CalTech or somewhere, Penn forgot, wore a beard and jazz shirts and called him Caddy, like he carried the guy's fucking golf bag around. All of which Penn hated, especially the beard. Guys with beards, what was that about? They think they look neat or what? As little boys had they gazed at guys with beards and thought, Wow, beards! I gotta get my chin into one of *those* suckers! Maybe they'd seen a comicbook ad: HEY KIDS!!! Never Have To Go Down On A Woman Again! Turn Your Face Into A Dog's Ass! Wonder Grow Your Own Beard Kit $5.99!

Art and his beard greeted Penn at the screen door with a manly whack on the shoulder that made his bursitis flare up momentarily.

—Caddy, *good* of you to come, Art said in his clipped New England style. And I do believe we have you to thank for our *surprise guest* tonight? He smiled, waggling his index and middle fingers in 'ironic' quotes.

Penn shrugged modestly. Oh, I don't know, he said, one does what one can. Penn had heard Art use that phrase once, and it seemed appropriate.

—Come come, Art admonished. You're not picking up an award here, *take* the credit. He led the way inside and called out, Muffy baby, Caddy's here.

—Down in a minute. Fix us some drinks, honey?

In the sunroom, sanded peg-and-groove floor, Swedish canvas furniture, grasscloth walls hung with cunt paintings, and a long window framing the sunset. Tonight's special: muted lavender tones offset with a bold slash of cerise and playful champagne accents. Penn sniffed appreciatively at the smell of cooking rolling in from the kitchen. Art took a bottle of Martini from a sea-chest with a whaling scene on it and organized the glasses.

—Smells good back there, said Penn.

Art laughed, his laugh just another word in his vocabulary he knew how to pronounce correctly. He nudged a rectangular space for the drinks between the neat stacks of books displayed on the table. Ah, yes, he said. Not a charge one would have leveled at Snakeboy. I am more than happy to say that our reptilian offspring has indeed shed his skin and emerged – *quelle surprise* – a human being of quite exceptional quality. In fact, he was observed ritually cremating his old epidermal layer in the yard last night. I only hope the gods appreciated it as much as we. But the metaphor is oddly inadequate for this particular metamorphosis, wouldn't you say?

He smiled in satisfaction at his inspirational turn of phrase, and poured the Martini neat, no messing it up with costly ice or lemon or olives or Noilly Prat or anything. They clinked glasses, sank back into the couch and watched the sun shiver into burning copper flags that colored the air in the room. Art shook his head, spoke quietly, basking in the dry precision of his own diction.

—A most welcome transformation. But, Caddy, by what strange alchemy? And there's something about the boy, I don't know, an *inner calm*, if I may be forgiven for the hackneyed phraseology. Some ineffable quality that defies facile categorization. We are intrigued, I confess! Just what exactly did you say to him? Ah, Caddy, use the coaster there? This table takes a stain real easy.

They were interrupted by Penn's mother coming in. She wore a long oatmeal linen dress with a wood bead necklace and her blond hair held up in a faded blue headscarf. Not for the first time Penn wondered how old Artie-boy had done so very nicely for himself. Margaret Penn had a trust fund, a beachfront cottage, some bulletproof stock, and knew how to drink lunch. Art Sloan's dowry consisted of a beard, male pattern baldness, the worst shirts in the world, and a rechargeable nasal hair trimmer.

—So, she laughed, welcome home! Art, honey, darling,

do go forage up some ice, would you? This Martini kind of lacks *drinkability*? Well! This is just so *nice*! Cad, we're just so-oo obligated to you . . . Hey, meet our cook! Ta-daa!

Penn turned toward the door, did a cartoon double-take that almost left whiz-lines in the air.

—Hey, Cad, said someone who was obviously not Snakeboy. Arthur Sloan III stood in the doorway, lit like an icon in a Russian church, catching the last of the sun. His punk hair gone, a clean golden fringe fell across a clear, untattooed face. He wore a white button-down Oxford shirt and pressed chinos, and an ovenmitt in the shape of a fish. He waggled it at Penn, working its mouth with his fingers. Dinner is served, he said in a ventriloquist's voice. They all laughed, Penn's amplified by astonishment.

—Hey hey, Arthur, he said, fly *threads*, bro!

The dinner was simple and good; home cooking like Penn thought he should remember but had probably never actually eaten at home before. Juicy fillet steaks flash-fried in butter and red Italian onions, and a warm salad of steamed vegetables. The table was full of talk and laughter, Arthur telling them how he'd re-enrolled in college that morning, making his mother clap her hands together in delight.

Penn couldn't keep his eyes off him. *Transformation* hardly carried it. *Something*, some cleansing, healing force of unimaginable power had started from the inside and hurricaned outward, affecting every part of him, body and soul. A kind of spiritual Toilet Duck that had really got up under his rim. Something profound and strong and, there was no other word for it, *good*. Every gesture, every word, every look was informed by it. It wasn't like he was bland or sanctimonious or pious; that would have been, in its own way, as bad as before. There was nothing, thank god, Christian about it.

No taint of religion at all. He was delightful, easy, witty company, and showed genuine interest in what Penn said, probably for the very first time. After the meal Arthur made his parents sit with coffees out on the deck while he and Penn did the dishes.

—Arthur, said Penn, shutting the door softly behind them, we have to talk. We really do.

—Well surely, said Arthur, pulling out a chair for Penn. They sat down at the scrubbed oak kitchen table, Arthur looking encouragingly at him while Penn struggled for the words, tapping his fingertips together to help him concentrate.

—Arthur, he said, what happened? Is this you? What's done this to you? Is it for real? It's nothing to do with what I said when I came over, is it? Is it? I don't get it . . .

Arthur smiled. Again Penn wondered at the good, simple smile, no complex undertow of irony or deceit. I do owe you some explanation, Arthur said, his voice quiet and steady. It must be pretty hard for you to understand. It's pretty hard for *me* to understand. I *can't* understand it. I haven't told anyone else, but you were there, so you should know the truth. No matter how crazy it sounds, I'm telling the truth as far as I can, okay? Not like I'm not going to leave anything out, it's just that I find it hard to describe what happened, like I know what happened but can't picture it, because I don't have the words, or the imagination, or anything to liken it to. And I can't *remember* it exactly, that *moment*. It's more like a memory of a memory. Okay? You ready for this?

Penn swallowed, nodded. The kitchen was silent except for bugs, attracted by the light, unwinding softly against the window like paper clockwork.

41

—It was in that apartment we fell into? Arthur continued. The kind of hippie place? I was, you know, going through the closets, looking for stuff to steal. I cannot believe I did that, you know? It's just so stupid, so *wrong* . . . anyway, I was looking through the guy's stuff, nothing valuable, just personal stuff, not much of anything, and I found this . . . *shoebox*.

He paused, indicating the size of a shoebox with his hands. Penn waited impatiently for him to go on, urging him with a nod of his head. Arthur's voice got even quieter.

—Just like a brown cardboard shoebox, with a label on the end, AMP or something, and a picture of a man's shoe . . . see, this sounds crazy to me when I put it into words like this. Okay, I picked it up, thinking there might be the guy's stash hidden inside it or something. There was something funny about the weight of it, something I can't describe. I mean, not like it was heavy or anything, just . . . anyway, that's when I opened it.

Arthur sat back, looking relieved, as if he'd got something over with, apparently not going to say any more. Penn squinted at him, head cocked on one side. *And?* he said. Arthur looked straight at him, his pale gray-blue eyes absolutely clear and still.

—I saw god, he said.

Penn snorted violently, slapped his hands on the kitchen table. Yeah, right. Sure you did. Spank my ass and call me Judy. God in a shoebox. What *style* was he? Wingtip? Oxford? Penny loaf . . . ? His laughter faltered to an embarrassed silence when he saw Arthur's eyes, how he was looking at him.

—I told you I don't have the words, Cad. God is as close as I can truthfully get. It's not like I saw a big old man in the

sky, or Jesus or anything. I didn't see a face, or a person, or
. . . *anything* I can describe to you. I saw, like I was really
seeing for the first time, and it totally changed me. Everything is new, Cad, everything. I guess it was like a light, but
a light that *had something in it.* I don't know. Something huge
and fantastic. And I can see how *good* everything is, how
close to perfect. This isn't making it any clearer, I know. It
was like, I don't know, when you open the windows on a
really great spring morning? And you fill your lungs with this
really fresh breeze right off the sea? Kind of like that, but
overpowering, as if you kept on breathing in and in and
never had to breathe out. And good, Cadogan, just so . . .
good. I know, I know, this is sounding like fundamentalist
radio. I'll shut up.

Penn watched as tears welled up in his brother's eyes.
Arthur laughed softly, wiped them away with a spotless
white handkerchief from the pocket of his chinos. I'm sorry,
Cad, he said. Crazy, right? And I'm afraid it gets crazier. He
stood up, a goofy wide-eyed grin on his face. Wanna come
outside? There's something else I discovered, maybe you
should see . . . a kind of side-effect . . .

He led the way out the kitchen door, down the creaking
steps to the hard sand. The sand shelved up behind the house
to the woods that shielded them from the PCH. In the
bloom of warm light from the kitchen, Penn saw his old
Schwinn bicycle, still chained to one of the stilts that
supported the house, all rusted up, tires rotten. He remembered with a sudden, terrible pang of something lost forever,
Christmas morning long ago, his dad pointing to the handle-
bar poking out between the drapes. Open the drapes, Cad!
And this beautiful shiny machine, red and black and chro-
mium, the most beautiful thing he'd ever seen, his heart

flying out to it. Riding it around and around in his pjs, ducking under the house and weaving between the stilts, grinning so much it hurt, his dad whooping him on from the porch every single time he passed. And now; this rust-spider's faint web, barely strong enough to trap a memory. *Go, Cad, go*, he whispered.

—Hey, Cad ... you okay? Arthur was sitting on the bottom step, motioning for Penn to join him.

—Uh, yeah, sure. Just, um, thinking. He hitched his pant knees so as not to bag them and sat down. Arthur scooped up a couple of pebbles from the ash-white sand, turned them over in his hand.

—Ready for this? he said, giving Penn a look. Penn, mystified into silence, shrugged. Okay, said Arthur. He closed his hands over the pebbles, slowly rotating them, keeping his gaze on Penn. It was starting to get a little awkward. Penn could hear the stones rubbing together. He started to get fidgety. Okay, said Arthur again, in exactly the same tone of voice. He opened his hands and brought the pebbles slowly up to Penn's face, cupped in his palm. Look, he whispered. The stones were completely transparent, like glass crystal beads. Penn watched dumbfounded as they began to turn milkily opaque, reverted to dull rock.

—There they go, said Arthur softly. It doesn't last long. He placed the pebbles on the step, wiped his palms on his thighs. Weird, huh?

Penn hooked his finger into his collar, stretched his chin up, cleared his throat. Yeah, it's weird, Arthur. They were quiet for a while. You haven't told anybody else about this, not anyone?

Arthur shook his head. No way. And no need.

—Good, said Penn. Don't.

Arthur grinned at him. Better join the folks. Watch the stars over the ocean for a while. They stood up. Penn pushed the door open for Arthur, snuck a look back at the pebbles, flicked them off the step with the toe of his shoe.

—So, he said on their way through the house, this, ah, shoebox. Still there, I guess?

FOUR

Feature Your Hurt Here

Penn couldn't get his head out of gridlock at Tischia's house next morning. He kept thinking about the damn shoebox. Kneeling on a yak-hair rug, contact sheets spread on the coffee table, the table she called an *occasional* table, like it was something else most of the time. He made an inventory of her stuff, to get his mind on track. Lumpy ethnic crockery and toys made of mud on a splintery shelf thing nailed up by Mexicans. A row of paperbacks enabling access to the hidden power within: *You Are Your First Child*; *The Dolphin Dances with the Tree*; *Knit a Forgiveness Quilt* (the one Tish had made him read); *Dear Me: Love Letters a Woman Can Write to Herself*. A photograph, in a plastic Garfield frame, of Tischia and Auburn Cord on Redondo Beach. Some new-age CDs. Now playing: *The Mormon Tabernacle Choir Sings Sacred Navaho Chants*.

Penn always had to take his shoes off so he didn't mark the woodblock floor or disturb the Zen-like sanctity of the place, and his knees ached from bending over the photographs. She kept asking him if he preferred this shot to that, or if her eyes weren't just a little squinty on this one, and what did he think? So it was a struggle to keep his mind on the job, and lucky Tischia was so self-absorbed she didn't notice his inattention. She was answering her own questions, anyway, commenting appreciatively on the way her hair or eyes or even – her word – *boobies* looked.

It seemed to Penn, gazing unconsciously at an image of Tischia's breasts surging up from the frothing surf, that there were two things here. Arthur's undoubted transformation, and this business about a shoebox. He felt ambivalent about the whole deal. Clearly Arthur had undergone a kind of deep-pan spiritual makeover, but just as clearly god could not reasonably have been waiting in a shoebox with that in mind. But then again, the Lord's Prayer; god moves in mysterious ways his wonders to something something. Arthur had been convinced, and very convincing, that the box had a key role in his rehab, so you never knew, right?

And why would Arthur invent something as risibly incredible as finding god in a shoebox? If he was angling for a spot on the Shuggy Kristiensen Cuckoo Couch, why had he left the box at the apartment? A *real* wacko would keep it clutched to his chest day and night and not let *anybody* have even a little peep, no sir, and hey, get those wires *off* of me. Pro-celebrity flakehood absolutely required just such a unique selling point, like the pager wired to the nipples or the wire wool in the jockeys. The shoebox would have had the necessary fetishistic brand value. It hadn't even occurred to Arthur to bring it with him.

And another thing. Arthur wasn't claiming to have seen Jesus, Buddha, or even Elvis at the gates of Graceland. He wasn't testifying, trying to get converts. He'd been appealingly vague, even a little embarrassed, about what he'd seen. In fact, it seemed like he didn't actually *know* what he'd seen. And, ultimately, it was Arthur's utter honesty that was the trickiest thing to deal with.

Penn moved in a world where sincerity was the murky

amniotic fluid all the half-truths swam around in, and where the truth had to be whatever you needed it to be. Nobody gave a shit for your honesty. This was not because they'd all inked a pact with the devil, like that Shakespeare guy. It didn't even mean they were bad people. It was just the way things worked, and it worked. Lies lubricated business, honesty was grit in the gears. Listening to Arthur simply speaking honestly as if he were incapable of lying had been close to a religious experience for Penn, something strange and disturbing.

The disappearing facial tattoo. That weird stuff with the pebbles. Trick of the light? Power of suggestion? Sleight of hand? Using soap? He sucked his breath in through his teeth and shook his head.

—You don't think so? said Tischia. Are you serious?

Penn blinked. Huh?

—The hair over the left shoulder?

—Sure.

—Sure what?

Penn grunted up onto the davenport, rubbing his knees. I smell like yak.

—Cadogan, she said crisply, I wish you could be more focused on this. It's important. She stood up and smoothed her leggings down, showing Penn a butt like an African carving. Was a time when a sharp whack across that butt with the flat of his hand would release the hidden power within them both, but that time, Penn realized, was now in its own glass case at the Smithsonian.

—I'm sorry, Tish. It's just this business about the suit. It really got to me, I guess. I kind of feel like it was my fault.

Even a month ago this kind of subtle approach would have yielded a conciliatory hair ruffle, segueing usefully into

48

a zesty little couch fuck. Today there was a new and ominous development.

—Cad, she said, her brow creased as if in thought, I've been thinking.

—Oh great, said Penn weakly. Good, thinking is good.

Tischia sat next to him on the davenport and accented her syllables with knee pats. I have been *thinking*, she said, that maybe, just *maybe*, what we're seeing here is how you could *use a little help*?

She said this in a wide-eyed whisper, mouthing the words clearly for any lipreaders in the room. Penn felt his tongue dehydrate. Help? he coughed.

Tischia held up her hands in a whoa-there gesture. Don't get into a right-wrong bind on this, okay? she said. Hey, I'm okay, you're okay (and, thought Penn, tomorrow is the first day of the rest of your life), so just flow with me on this, and then we'll take a time out, okay? And you can have the space to feature your hurt. Okay. She moved for dramatic effect to the mirror, avoiding Penn's eyes, concentrating on her recitation, brow puckering cutely. I am increasingly clear that, what with my career path looking real good right now, that it may be an appropriate time to, kind of, you know, reassess the level of support that, like, I'm getting from you.

Penn stood up, flapping his hands. Waitwaitwaitwait, he said. I am *way* ahead of you on this and no way am I going to split a deal with Manley Elmhurst on this. Noooo way. So, this was it, thought Penn, the old icepickeroonie between the shoulderblades. Manley Elmhurst was Tischia's previous agent, the guy who probably sent her the flowers on the white *decor* piano. Maybe even the white *decor* piano, for all Penn knew.

49

Tischia pushed up at her fringe with her fingertips. Cadogan, I think it would be appropriate for you to take on board that Manley and me have had my contract real professionally analyzed and there is no – *What had the guy said?* – let or, or hindrance? To me pursuing my career. Like, as I see fit. She smiled at him in the mirror, expecting plaudits for her keynote address.

—What you're saying is, said Penn, as controlled as he could, that after all my considerable emotional and financial investment, this Manley guy sleazes right up into bed with us? And I get to take it in the ass and chew a little pillow? Excuse me, am I on track here, or did I miss something?

—Cadogan, don't be so gross. This is coming from a pretty warped perspective, but that's okay, you're featuring your hurt. And I am in a listening place for your upsetness. Manley will not compromise our relationship, which is as important to me as it is to us, right? My concern is I need the best team around me at this time. Play to strengths. My career is way too important . . . than to entrust with just one individual. My request is that this is an empowering thing. Take a time out, think it over, and call me tomorrow, okay?

Penn, too furious to trust himself to say anything else, went to the door, clenching and unclenching his fists rapidly, feeling his nails bite into his palms. Tischia was pushing her hair about in the mirror, focused on achieving the best effect. Now she was, like, totally clear on the relationship situation.

—Left shoulder, see? she said, smiling at her reflection.

Penn went out and closed the door softly behind him. I do not believe I just let that happen, he said out loud. Manley fucking Elmhurst? What is happening to my life? Boiling over with self-righteous indignation, he turned and beat on the door. Tischia opened it, holding his deck shoes between finger and thumb. He sagged visibly. Uh, thanks, he said. Tischia giggled cutely and shut the door.

Penn drove to Le Park and Steven got him a table with the same zip code as the bar as a special favor.

—What is happening to my life, Steven?

Steven twisted open the bottle of water for him. My guess, he said, someone with tits is turning it to shit. Have the Mystery Meat in Fava Bean and Chianti Sauce. Nobody else is, and it's beginning to look like your life. No charge if you look like you're enjoying it.

Penn chewed his food without even bothering to scope the place out, engrossed in his thoughts, obsessed by the image of Manley Elmhurst with his horrible silver hair sleazing up to Tischia, arms full of flowers and pianos. He shuddered.

—One second?

Penn looked up from his Mystery Meat to see Dean Mance apparently showing him what a cellphone looked like. Penn gazed at it glassily, then up at Mance. He was a tall guy with thinning hair who people took for an intellectual on account of his height, architect's eyeglasses, and the way he always wore black Donna or Calvin. Dean Mance was about as intellectual as a sack of two-headed snakes.

—I just fielded a call from Manley Elmhurst? Says he has exclusive representation of Tischia Burke White. What's going on here, Cad? This is a need-to-know situation. And what you need to know is we're tabling paper at Paramount Friday and I'm not going in on one leg on this.

Penn got to his feet and pulled out a chair for Mance. Jesus, Dean, that asshole, really, sit down . . . please . . .

Mance shook his head. Uh-uhn. Core this out for me.

—I'll get it cleared. Don't field any more calls from

Elmhurst. The guy's dreaming. He's sick. You're talking to me. White is my property, and my guys are down Elmhurst's throat as of right this second, the fuck. Nothing's changed, Dean, take a me pill on this . . .

Mance looked at his watch, shooting it out from under a heavy white silk cuff.

—NET, Cad. I can't devote any more time to this aspect right now. Get this anchored up this pm, or you'll be signing snow come Friday, okay?

Left alone at his table, Penn's face grotesqued through anger, frustration, and disbelief, like one of those many-moods-of photo spreads. *Any tea?* What the fuck did that mean?

—You're wasted in agency work, Cad, said Steven, coming by to collect the plate. That facial dexterity is your ticket to moviedom's highest accolades.

Penn sighed. Tell me, Steven, since you're hanging ten at the crest of the zeitgeist, what does *any tea* mean?

—It's like this big thing with holes they use to catch fish?

—What? Oh, n-e-t, right, it's letters. I knew that. So?

Steven used the eyebrow pinch again. I got it, he said. Not Enough Time. It's a brush-off acronym. Congratulations! You've made it! Penn's face lit up for a second, as he banked the information, then he fell silent. *So*, said Steven with a cough. Anyway already, how was your brother's birthday?

—Huh? Oh. You know how some things in life are just too weird to begin to think about?

—What, like those tiny black flies that live in icecubes? Or how you never ever see the same make of hot-air dryer twice no matter how many toilets you go into?

—Huh? Let me come at this from another angle. Ever juggle four pounds of shit in a two-pound bag?

—Tell you what; eat some cake.

—I *think*, said Penn, that on mature reflection I shouldn't have anyone for a client that's reading *Making YOU a Powerful Place to Be* by Dr Ira Fucking Nussbaum MD. I intend to have it drawn up as a rider. I may even sue the smug fuck for being instrumental in destroying my life totally.

Penn picked up his BMW and headed out toward Tuscadero Street. Felt obligated to check the place out, right? This was family. And god knows he needed a break from busting his brain about Tischia. And Manley Elmhurst and his lovely hair. Especially that. He parked in the Z-Mart lot and walked the two blocks to the Porn Baron, casually retraced his escape route from the fat guy with the baseball bat.

Citizens on the street looked suspiciously legit, carrying grocery sacks like it was a Richard Scarry illustration. A foam-flecked wino shuddering in the gutter contributed warming genre-scene detail. Penn wondered briefly where these guys shopped for clothes; dirty orange plaid slacks, illness-colored undershirts and fraying house slippers. Was J. Crew's struggle for nothing?

Penn, meanwhile, wearing the nearest his closet got to street style, looked like he was taking time out from buffing his yacht to cruise for sushi. He paused to pretend to look in the window of an electronics store, *Famous Name Car Sterio's At $$$ Below List*, secretly using the reflection to scope the street, like he'd seen in the movies.

He edged down the alley, stink of cat piss he hadn't

noticed before, past the muffler shop yard, casually swung over the fence, slipped between two-floor apartment blocks dense with tangles of bad graffiti, windows plywooded up. He peered into the hippie pad. Dark. Nobody home. Maybe. The window was closed but he could see the catch hadn't been hooked over, just like they'd left it.

He walked on around the corner to the street that led back up to Tuscadero. Some kids were smacking the windshield of a trashed Datsun pickup, taking it in turns to swing the pipe. Penn went into the apartment block and knocked on the first door on the right, the one with suns painted all over. He could always make an excuse, wrong number, whatever.

—Ain't there, said a voice. Penn turned to see a skinny kid zippering up after taking a leak on the stairs. Just gone to the store. Be back directly. Need anything? Off-street prices.

The kid hadn't looked up. All Penn could see was a dirty purple LA Lakers baseball cap. The kid adjusted his crotch. No, said Penn quickly. No thanks. I'll come by later. He skipped back around the corner, pulled up the window, folding back a fingernail sickeningly, slid inside, heart racing, thinking *This is really stupid*. He half turned to leave, changed his mind, pirouetted back, did it all over again like he was Martha Graham on PBS. *Jesus*, he hissed, impatient with himself. He stared stupidly at a poster on the wall, some illegible psychedelic shit, took a breath. Okay. Let's go to work.

In the next room was a sleeping bag, some dried plant stalks in ordered little heaps on the floor, an open book with some Chinese writing. Penn saw none of this. He stepped straight to the closet and slid the door open. Dayglo paisley shirts and empty wire hangers on the rail; on the floor a pile of newspapers with a shoebox on top. Penn dropped to his knees, biting his lower lip in concentration.

There was a label on the end with a picture of a black Oxford shoe, and the word AMPAR. Someone had scribbled the shoe size on the label in pencil. Penn held his breath, lifted the box. Something startlingly odd about the feel of it made him put it back quickly, wiping his palms on his slacks. Arthur had said something about that, hadn't he? He shivered involuntarily. Well, he said to himself, do *something*, or get the hell out of here. Piss or get off the pot.

Very gently, he lifted the box again. It was almost like there was water inside, moving from one end to the other, but very slowly. Only it wasn't as heavy as water; in fact the box felt empty in terms of weight. But when he moved it there was this resistance, and the balance shifted. Like a friction toy, you push it until it moves by itself, kind of like that, or water. Or like nothing else at all. Bizarre, totally.

Out in the hallway he heard a key scratch in the lock. Suddenly resolved, he tucked the box under his arm and ran back through to the window, sprinted away up the alleyway.

Back up on the street he caromed right off a big fat guy coming out of the electronics store, a big fat black guy with a goatee, a knit cap, and insectoid sunglasses. Penn was trying to regain his balance without dropping the box when the fat guy said, Shee-it, motherfucker, don't I know you?

All Penn knew was, everything he wanted was somewhere else, instantaneously. *Fuck*, he said under his breath, and skipped into the street, looking for a break in the traffic. The fat guy came after him. Penn, with the calm reason of a rabbit in a headlamp beam, leaped back down the alley. The fat guy, unfairly fleet of foot, caught up, smashed him against the wall, held his neck at arm's length like it was a pencil, smacked his fist up hard into Penn's gut. Penn doubled up, slid to the ground, acrid sting of bile in his mouth.

—Know what you is? asked the fat guy conversationally. Yo' what we call a repeat customer, cave boy. Get special treatment on account of your loyalty. *Personal* attention. He put his foot on Penn's face, ground it into the cat piss and grit. Gimme the watch, motherfucker. He grabbed Penn's arm, looked at the watch. What is *this* shit?

—Rolex, grunted Penn.

—*You* are one sad motherfucker. I shit better Rolex. He kicked Penn in the ass, hard and accurate. Penn straightened his legs in reflex spasm, squirming on the ground, and the guy kicked him in the belly. Penn felt something hot squirt out his mouth and nose. The fat guy leaned over and whispered, What's in the box? Penn hugged it to his chest, gasping for breath. Hey, biscuit boy! the fat guy shouted. I ask a question.

—Shoes? Penn whispered, his mouth clogged, sharp and foul. He felt the shoe on his cheek again, twisting, grinding his face.

—They better be *Rolex* shoes, motherfucker. I have to tell you, I be real into that gratification shit.

Desperate, Penn shut his eyes tight, opened the box. Immediately, he felt the foot slide off his face. He counted to ten, whimpering, fumbled the lid back, opened his eyes to slits. The fat guy was just standing there motionless, looking at his hands like he'd never seen them before, mouth hanging open. Penn wrenched himself into a sitting position, guts feeling like someone had wound them out on a stick.

The fat guy's shoulders began to shake. He sank gently to his knees, hands going up to his head. Penn spit, wiped his face with his hand. The fat guy had taken off his sunglasses and his eyes shone like they were wired, wet with tears. His mouth split into a huge, blinding grin.

—God, he said, I am a son of a bitch. S'okay, man, I ain't gone rush you no more, on the real. My ass is so out. Wanna grab some help here? He stood up and offered Penn his hand. Penn flinched, shook his head. Listen, the big guy said, I'm gone do the right thing here, man, I'm gone make shit cool between us, okay? You just hang yo' ass here, I be right back.

He touched Penn gently on the shoulder and walked up onto the street, turning back to give a reassuring wave, his soft chuckle building to a deep laugh that echoed down the alley. Penn cradled the box in his hands, feeling its emptiness shift slowly, like a miniature tide, while his head cleared. Wait here? What was he, crazy? He struggled painfully to his feet, holding the box carefully under his arm, and limped back up to the street, bent double. He attracted no interest staggering back to the Z-Mart lot; minimal percentage in re-mugging the sorry fuck.

He was dry-heaving against his car when someone yelled, Hey, Ralph Lauren! Penn ducked inside but the fat guy was already there and pulling the door open.

—Your stereo, he said, grinning. And I'd like to pay for the window?

Penn, dazed, took the radio. Thanks, he said. Uh, they billed me three hundred fifty . . . for the window . . .

—No problem. Gimme couple days. Come by the pool-room back up on the Tusc, okay? Day after tomorrow. I don' know *what* I'm thanking you for, like . . . wow . . . boom shit happenin' . . . uh . . . and I'm real sorry fo' bangin' on you. Gut be killin' you fo' couple days. Wha's yo' name, man, calling you motherfucker now we vibin' an' shit.

—Cad Penn.

—That a name or you just clearing your throat?

Penn grinned in spite of himself, passed him a card from his wallet with trembling fingers. Cellphone number, he croaked. Address is wrong.

—Stay cool. Don' intend draggin' my black ass round fo' afternoon tea. Yeah, real substantial shit, Mr Cad-o-gan Penn. Ass-ociates, huh? Shit, I *knew* you wasn't a nigger. He grabbed Penn's hand and did a complex soulbrother thing with it, chuckling at Penn's ineptness. Tyler Dupree, he said. Later, homeboy.

Penn watched him go over to help a shaky little old guy who'd dropped his groceries loading the trunk of his Chevrolet. This obese thug, Penn thought, a moment ago kicking the living shit out of him, now chasing oranges for a senior citizen. Penn stared at the box in his lap as if the sheer concentrated laser force of his gaze would be enough to reveal the secret within.

Just what kind of miracles could this thing perform for him? Three and a half Cs? He snorted. Wouldn't even pay for the label. Wouldn't even buy the pencil that wrote the shoe size on the label. He stroked the box on his lap and laughed, a sly and secret laugh that only he heard.

FIVE

The More There Is, the Better It Smells

Tischia Burke White was not best pleased by the sight of Penn on her doorstep, just when she was lipsticked up for her girlfriend Auburn Cord. She was wearing her Versace stretch jeans with the lace-trimmed rips, and a tight Guess jeans jacket that showed off a delectable strip of flat, tan midriff below a lot of cleavage trimmed with white bra froth. Auburn had just landed a speaking in a Dabney Coleman dramedie, and they were going to trawl Giorgio's and then to Spago's to sin out on chocolate cake. She didn't need another sob-session with Penn right now.

—Will you please make this quick? she said, opening the door.

Penn didn't look too great at all. The side of his face was all grazed up and he was hunched over like he hurt to walk, carrying a box under his arm. He went right over to the couch and sat with the shoebox on his lap.

—Have you been hit by a truck or what? she said. You look yucky-pucky. Hey, your shoes, remember? Listen, I'm meeting Auburn Cord right now?

—Yeah, right, he said, kicking his shoes off. Tish, I got you something. A gift. To help us start over.

Tischia frowned at the box. What, like *guy* shoes? What is this? You look really yucky.

—I'm okay. You're okay, I'm okay, and I got something real special just for you, said Penn, intriguing it up. Something . . . *valuable*. And it's just for you. C'mon over here. Take a peek. You won't be sorry.

Tischia made a kind of little impatient clucking sound but Penn could see she was hooked. I swear, Cad, if this is like a puppy or something, she said, sitting opposite him, swinging her legs gracefully to one side and clutching her see-thru vinyl purse with the plastic dolphins in it. Penn laughed and slid the box toward her thinking, a real occasion for an occasional table.

—Believe me, he said, it's nothing like a puppy. Take a me pill. You looking? I don't want you to miss this. Look right in the box now . . .

He closed his eyes and took off the lid. Nothing seemed to happen for a long time. When he heard sobbing he carefully replaced the lid and opened his eyes. Tischia Burke White had her face in her hands and was blubbing like a baby. Great shuddering slobbery boo-hoos. He let her sit there for a while, her shoulders shaking, then moved to her side.

—Tish? Hey, Tish honey?

She took a tissue from her purse, dabbed her eyes. Her purse fell off her lap onto the floor. S'okay, she said. Leave it. She was taking in massive lungfuls of air and breathing it out slowly through her mouth. Gritty trails of mascara sparkled on her cheeks. Wow, she exhaled, turning to look at him and breaking into a smile. Wow. She wiped her cheeks and laughed. I spent two hours smearing this stuff on, and now look at me.

—Hey, no problemo. Can I build you a drink?

She shook her head. But you go ahead. Please.

Penn went to the drinks cabinet and poured a six-ounce glass of Black Label, keeping an eye on Tischia. Her face was just glowing, like someone tripped a switch in the back of her head. She was looking around the room, smiling at things, saying *Wow* over and over. When she looked at Penn she smiled at him, too. The kind of smile he'd seen a couple of times before recently. He gulped the Scotch back.

—I told you it was a special gift, he said, baring his teeth as the malt afterburn kicked in.

—Oh, Cad, she said, I can't explain this, but this isn't your gift.

—Huh?

She stood up and came toward him. Give me your hands, Cad, look at me. She took his hands in hers and he looked into her eyes. It was strangely uncomfortable, like it had been with Arthur. She seemed to see right into him, but without judging what she saw. Like a baby's eyes, only kinder, or more understanding maybe, but with that same unsettling penetrating intelligence. It wasn't yours to give, Cad, she said. It's nothing you can own . . . it's not, like, I don't know, a puppy or something. She laughed, realizing how ridiculous she was sounding to herself. A beautiful, light sound he'd not heard her make before.

—Right, said Penn blinking. But we ought to talk about things? You know, like the future?

She gently let his hands go, fingertips lingering for a moment. Everything's going to be all right, she said. It'll be a little different than we thought, but it's going to be okay, okay?

Penn hit himself with another Black Label, his mind swiveling crazily. Something was very badly off track somewhere. What different? he said. How okay?

—Everything's so . . . *beautiful*, she said, gazing out the window at the palms and the houses opposite.

Penn interrupted before she started singing Ray Stevens songs. Yeah, right, he said enthusiastically. Beautiful. Absolutely. So, are we still an item? Can we forget this crap about Manley Elmhurst? I have to get this anchored up soonest or we'll be signing snow come Friday.

Tischia turned from the window, and the light blurred her blond hair into a saint-like golden halo. Another award-winning lighting effect, thought Penn, remembering Arthur's icon-like appearance.

—Cad, forgive me, but there is no way things aren't going to change, not now. It's like I've been . . . *lying* to you all the time . . .

—*All* the time? What do you mean?

—I'm sorry, Cad. Please, sit down. Listen. I don't love you. I'm sorry, Cad. I *never* loved you. I just used you to lever a better contract out of Manley, and I can't lead you on anymore. I really set you up, and I've been living a lie. It has to stop. I wish you, really, all the happiness in the world, but it's not fair to let you think I can share it with you, okay?

Penn was devastated. This was *not* the show he'd bought the ticket for. Share it with me? he said dumbly. What, this means you're with Manley Elmhurst, totally?

Tischia laughed. No, Cad. I'm with Manley Elmhurst, like, un-totally.

She knelt in front of him. Penn, slumped on the couch, stared into her cleavage with the horrible realization it was like ogling a sister. I'm with me for a time, she said quietly. I have to look at my life, think it through. I think I wasted so much of it already. I feel . . . that the me you knew is like somebody else. It's like I can recognize her, but she's so *distant* . . .

Penn gripped the glass in frustration, slopping Johnnie Walker on his pants. *Distant?* he croaked. Tish, this is *Nick Nolte*, for crissakes! How distant can you be?

—Cad, look at me. Do I look the same as I did ten minutes ago?

No, he thought, she looks as much like her old self as Arthur had looked like his. Sure, her clothes were the same, but in a way that only pointed up what had changed. Everything. Everything that made a person what they're made of. There was a naturalness to her movements that made her previous gracefulness seem like working the pole in a titty bar. And her face was like – he labored for a metaphor – like the sun coming out of a cloud. Younger and older, more innocent and wiser, all at once. Open. Happy. Good. Like a sister he really really loved. Loved like a sister. *Damn.*

—No, he said defeatedly. No, Tish, you don't. I guess this scene just didn't play through like my script. I got the wrong sides. Penn glanced at the box. I kind of thought, he said sadly, this thing would get us back on track again, clear away the crap between us, bring us closer. It's done that, but not like I expected. Not like I wanted. Penn gave a deep, heartfelt groan, and worked his sore jaw with his hand. Tish took his empty glass and put it on the table.

—You're not going to start *tidying* or anything, are you? he said. I mean, don't you even want to ask me any *questions*, about the box, or whatever? You don't seem inquisitive. I did a miracle here for you and you don't even seem curious. You haven't looked at the box since I closed it. That's what I call curious.

—It's a shoebox, Tischia smiled. Why would I want to look at it? I have no need for curious, Cad. I was curious before I looked in the box. Mildly. And I have to tell you that you can't take credit for what happened here. Cadogan Penn had nothing to do with this. Your box is a shoebox. It's really, like, irreverent, in a way. Do I mean that? Irrelevant? Like it's not what matters. You're the one who should be curious, right?

Penn found himself reaching out to touch her hair. It was so beautiful, framing her beautiful face. He couldn't have a hissy fit with a girl like that. Well, he said, I guess I am, Tish. Was it, like Jesus or something, or a blinding Zen-like void? Can you describe for me what you actually saw?

Tischia crinkled up her nose, giving him a lopsided smile. I can't even begin. It was like . . . nothing else. So much like nothing else I'm not even sure if I saw anything. Maybe bright light is closest, but it was something I think I felt more than saw. All I know is, everything is suddenly, like, *good* . . . I don't know how to put it. Remember how I was like really anti-value judgments? It's like I know what *good* really is now, and it isn't an alternative. *Stuff* is good. This couch, the floor . . . you. The stuff everything's made of is *good*. I don't know if I'll ever think this through, but I don't feel I need to, for myself. It's like trying to think through the sky or something. If you're inquisitive, why don't you look? The *box* is yours, I guess . . .

Penn pushed a hand back through his hair, wincing a little as he stretched his grazed cheek. I don't know, Tish, he said, gazing unseeingly into the middle distance. Not yet. For now, what am I going to tell Dean Mance?

Tischia leaned up and kissed his cheek. It felt cooler right away. Whatever you do, Cad, you'll do okay. Just, I don't know, find another property to represent. Plenty more fish in the sea. I'm sorry, but I'm not part of it anymore. I can't pretend I am.

She went to the door and opened it for him, with the smile that made it impossible for him to be angry at her. She looked so goddam happy, so . . . beautiful. In her own way. Like the summer sunshine . . .

—Take care, Cad.

Penn stood up uncertainly, feeling like he might cry. My life is turning to sh—

She reached out and put her finger to his lips. Shhhh. And don't forget your shoes this time. You want the box, or will you wear them now?

Penn pushed his feet into his shoes and picked up the box, feeling the subtle movement inside. Do you have any twine? he asked. I don't need the lid falling off and giving me a life change before I get home, giving my money to shrubs. She tied up the box with some sparkly gift twine, finishing it off with a neat little bow. Penn looked at her with a longing and sense of loss he hadn't felt since, he couldn't think. I really did love you, he said, realizing as he said it that it was only *now* that he really loved her.

She passed him the box. I'm real sorry, she said, but it's better this way. Well, it's not like there's a choice anymore. It's like all one thing. Take care, Cad . . .

Penn stood in the porch with the dead weeds brushing the top of his head. He couldn't bear to look at her, so happy and beautiful. And his gut still ached. Listen, he said. You notice any, uh, side-effects, weird stuff happening, you call me, okay? I'm here to help.

The door clicked shut. Now he remembered. Last time he'd felt that overwhelming sense of loss was when he'd stuffed his candy-apple red '67 Corvette into an eighteen-wheeler on the 405. Now *that* had been a pisser. They don't counsel for 'vette-loss, even in LA. He'd had to shoulder up and pull through all by himself. He could do it again. He was learning. Life was hard.

On the way back to his Marina Del Rey office and swank bachelor pad, Penn cued slowly through what Tischia had said. There'd been some good bankable stuff there. Something about finding a new property to represent. Something about him not being able to give what was in the box because it wasn't something you could have. Maybe true, if he could understand it. But maybe he could, like, *represent* it, whatever it was. Yeah. Take a legitimate cut. This was what he did, so play to strengths, right?

His parking slot was occupied by a bigwheel offroader. He parked somewhere else, cursing, climbed the stairs that led up from the beach and buzzed his neighbor. Billy opened the door wearing Wile E. Coyote shorts and an outsize foam stetson.

—Howdy, Cad.

—You got the wrong bay again, Billy. Means I get a call later from the guy whose place I had to take. He has to park on the next street. Get it? It's kind of like a knock-on effect. Eventually somewhere down the line some sap has to park on a grade crossing and his kids get crushed by a train, because you didn't park in your own slot. I hope you can live with that.

He left Billy working that out, scratching his belly, and let himself into his apartment. A duplex decorated in black and white, with bright red wall-to-wall. On this floor, bedroom and bathroom in the back, separated by the kitchenette from his comfort zone; the living room, sliding patio doors onto the balcony where he tanned and watched the beach. Open fireplace, which he never used, leather couch, coffee table, chrome-framed photographs of muscle cars, Camaro, Trans-Am, Corvette. A tan BarcaLounger set in front of the TV, ringed by a scum-tide of VCR cassettes and magazines: *Variety*, *Road & Track*, *Lui*, *Sports Illustrated Swimwear Issue*. Ripped box of salt-free sourdough pretzels, empty Californian wine bottles. Open staircase up to his office area on the mezzanine; black ash-finish desk with a phone/fax deal and a half-assembled Revell Mustang model kit gathering dust. Telescope on a tripod by the copper-tinted window looking out over the ocean, joggers plodding heavily over the sand. Penn dropped his keys on the desk, punched the message button.

—Cad, this is Steven. If you're there listening to this, don't pick up, okay? Uh, Cad, this is difficult for me to say. Well, actually, I just have to move my mouth and the words come out. Oh sure, it looks easy, but that's the magic of the actor's art. Okay. I've been aware for some time that my career as an actor has not been getting the kind of gung-ho support that I think it warrants. I have no complaints about your valuable support for me as a wait-person, however, and I'd like this part of our relationship to continue. Just until someone dies at the carwash. So, Cad, what I'm saying is, strike me off your call-sheet, okay? Oh, and thanks for the gratuity. Just so you know, I'm putting half into no-load mutual funds and hitting Vegas with the rest. See you on the sidewalk sometime.

Penn placed the shoebox carefully on the desk and stared at it while he did some focused head time. He sat in his canvas director's chair, lit a new Monte Cristo and blew the smoke down his nose. He thought some more. He picked up the rear axle assembly from the Mustang kit and spun the wheels. In the depths of his blue-gray eyes a spark of animal cunning ignited, and guile lines appeared at the corners of his mouth and eyes. And the more he thought, the deeper these lines got. He made a brief call to his mother to check that Arthur's facial tattoo hadn't reappeared. Then he called Dean Mance's office.

Dean Mance put Penn on hold while his line at Tri-Star told him that Sony was so dead in the water they'd given their green light to a traffic cop. Mance yokked it up, Ha ha, fanning himself with his Rolodex, because the guy was flying some good flags right now. Mance waved goodnight to Sandi, his PA, while the guy finished talking up his new Gotham brownstone. Like Cosby's place, only with four walls. Ha ha. After the call Mance shuffled some papers on his desk, made some notes on his call-sheet, and filled his Mont Blanc. Then he thumbed the hold button onto hands-free and stretched back in his Per Lundqvist recliner, the leather creaking reassuringly.

—Hey, Cad, how's it flowing? he said through a yawn.

—Hey, Dean, squawked Penn's voice from the box on the desk. Fluid enough to suck through a straw.

Mance inserted a pinkie into his left nostril and probed thoughtfully. So tell me, am I getting it in the ass from you or Elmhurst? You can understand how little I care. Just as long as it's not both of you up there.

—Ha ha. Let me come from outside the square on this. I have a property that will change your world, a deal you can't lose, and you're going to love me for the rest of your life. All you have to do is give me thirty before you wax the floor tonight.

Mance eased out his pinkie, turned it in the light. He'd heard this kind of pitch before. Penn, he said, this is the sound of a dying man.

—Okay, what can I say? I tell you what I can say. I'm so excited on this I will pay you a thousand bucks just to look at it. Up front, in old bills. And you haven't heard that one before. This is all-new.

Mance leaned forward and picked up the phone. You pulling my taffy? It's kind of late in the day for frat-house pranks.

—Nope, said Penn. Gospel truth.

—A thousand bucks, huh? Well, you wore me down, Cad. I have a window at – he consulted his agenda – six. Bring the money, and a major capacity for disappointment. And what is this, uh, *property*, exactly?

—That's what I'm paying you to find out, Dean.

Mance replaced the phone and raised his bushy eyebrows. A thousand bucks just to doze through a showreel? He uncapped the tiny silver bottle he kept on a chain around his neck and tapped a little white powder onto the back of his hand, snorked it up, licked it clean. Then he dialed Auburn Cord's personal number and told her machine he'd pick her up at eight as planned, and to wear something black and barely large enough for a small Tiffany pin. He should be inside her apartment at twelve and her underwear at five past if that thousand bucks stood up for him like he envisaged. Nothing like diamonds and pink champagne at the Bowl for hanging pussy off your johnson. Thank god some American values proved impervious to AIDS and the New Puritanism.

Exactly at five before six, Penn swung the BMW down Doheny, where Mance took office space in a Spanish-style serviced building with a glittering tile mural covering one exterior wall. He parked in the visitor's bay and an automatic door sucked him into the airconditioned lobby.

He checked the place out while the uniformed guy on the desk put down a plastic rabbit he was levering open with a pocket knife and called his name up. On the wall between the elevators was an edge-lit perspex panel with the names of the lessees cut into it, glowing reassuringly. This, Penn knew, was a mark of real class, evidence of long-term commitment and solidity. Only office building he'd ever taken space in had one of those cheap lobby boards with plastic letters pushed into it, and somebody kept rearranging all the letters into off-color phrases.

Someday he'd have an office in a building again, instead of an apartment. A building like this, with shiny terrazzo floors and a glass table with the trades on it and six-cushion ottomans and elevators. Only bigger. With tomorrow's trades. A wall full of elevators, some going sideways, and two guys fixing toy rabbits. Full-time.

—Okay, Mr Penn, fifth floor on your left and *damn* this bunny, said the guy on the desk as the toy's head ricocheted across the lobby floor. The bell pinged and Penn took the elevator to the fifth floor, carrying the box under his arm. The corridor was broad, fleck berber carpeted, sepia prints of Old Burbank on the walls, which always reminded Penn of Hiroshima for some reason. All that empty space. He pushed his fingers back through his hair and opened the door into Mance's office. Mance took three rooms overlooking the street, decorated in solid varsity style. A massive abstract painting with bits of crockery stuck to it said, Hey, Dean Mance knew from art. Mance was shouldering into his big jacket, his back to Penn.

70

—Put the money on the desk, he said, and walked into his screening room without looking around. Penn took the envelope from his pocket and kissed it, raising his eyes in prayer. This was his emergency apocalypse stash he'd never before taken out from behind the bathroom cabinet. He put it on the desk and followed Mance, who'd stretched out in the first of three rows of leather chairs in front of the wallmounted Sony flat-screen.

—Rock my world, Cad, he said ironically, thumbing a remote that simultaneously lowered the blackout blinds and powered up soft floor-level lighting. He linked his long fingers behind his head and said, Then we can talk about Tischia Burke White for five minutes, and you leave me to invest your thousand bucks as I deem wise, and in a week or so Sandi highlights me a sad little clipping about your body being found slumped over a toilet somewhere with pills all over.

Penn made an effort to chuckle, and took the chair next to Mance, the box on his lap, giving him a spookily unsettling smile, his face dimly underlit. Mance shrank back a little in his seat.

—Jesus, Cad, you look like shit. Been auditioning for a Turkish fuck-fight movie?

—Okay, Dean, I've paid the fee. The next thirty minutes are mine, right?

Mance frowned. Ye-ah . . . he said, eyeing the shoebox with its glittery gift twine.

—Good, said Penn encouragingly. Good. Because, like I said, I have a piece of business here that will change your life. But first we need to agree on some conditions.

—Uh-*uhn*, interrupted Mance. I'm agreeing to jack shit except sitting here with my feet in my shoes for the next – he shot his Oyster from his shirtcuff – twenty-six minutes.

Penn smiled at him. Oh, but these are conditions you'll like, because they're for your benefit. And it's all a gentleman's agreement. No paperwork, just verbal, okay? Mance narrowed his eyes suspiciously at the concept of a gentleman's agreement. So, the arrangement is this, Penn continued. I've paid you the money for you to look at what I have. When you've looked at it, *if* you agree it's the greatest thing you've ever seen, you give me my money back. And tomorrow, if it's *still* the greatest thing you've ever seen, you go to the bank and you get me one hundred thousand dollars and you bring it to my apartment at noon and you give it to me. With a signed letter of introduction to Ed Usher, which I've drafted out here, based on what you see tonight.

Penn took the letter from his pocket and let Mance read it. Mance snorted, an amused sneer on his lips. Oh, right, he said heavily. A hundred large. And this buys me your, uh, property.

—Nope, smiled Penn, this buys you zip-ola. Jack shit. You'll give me the hundred large because you're one grateful son of a bitch, and you promised. Call it a simple gesture of good faith.

Mance laughed. A crazy-horses, high-pitched laugh. Call it fucking crazy. You been eating way too many Happy Meals, Cad. Let's just hypothesize wildly for a moment. Work with me on this. Let's suppose, hey, devil's advocate, that I think what you've shown me is a crock of shit. Let's suppose that is the albeit unlikely outcome. What, pray, then?

Penn shrugged. That's when you win. You get *another* thou – he patted his jacket pocket – and I get to chew barbiturates and hump the toilet.

—Let's see if I got this straight. He repeated what Penn had just said, very slowly and emphatically as if he were having difficulty getting his head around it. Penn nodding supportively. Mr Penn, he said, confidence is a great thing in this business. A great thing, widely admired. And I'm about to teach you the small but crucial difference between being confident and being yodeling fucking crazy. But I'd like to make it clear that even if I *like* what you're going to show me, what the fuck it is, you still lose, right? Even if I really *really* like it, and want a part of the action. It has to be the greatest thing I've ever seen for me to lose this deal. I have to use those words.

—Absolutely. It has to knock you out. Like I told you, you can't lose on this deal. Mance laughed unpleasantly at this. But, said Penn, raising his index finger, you have to *promise* to keep the agreement.

Mance repeated the word as if it had a bad taste. *Promise?*

Penn nodded again. From the heart.

Mance whistled through his teeth, shaking his head. Jesus, Cad, I don't know . . . okay, I guess so.

—Say it, then . . . *I promise* . . .

Mance mimicked the tone in Penn's voice, wagging his head from side to side, *I promise* . . .

—Nonononono, said Penn. From the heart. Real simple. Let me coach you on this. You really *want* that two thousand bucks. Got it? Mance took a breath, focused on the two large, made the promise.

Penn undid the bow, shut his eyes, and opened the box.

Penn was still in his robe next day when the door chimes did their cheery chimey thing. He checked the kitchen clock. Ten-thirty. He padded barefoot to the door and squinted through the peephole. *My man*, he said, and slid back the bolts.

—Hey, Dean. How's it flowing?

Dean Mance stood grinning in the hallway. He wore a tieless white shirt, black Levis, desert boots, a huge smile, and carried a box under his arm.

—Hey, Cad. Like pear butter off a hot muffin. I'm early, I know, but I have a lot to do today. It's like the first day for me. I can't explain it. I just want to get out there. I thought this was kind of an appropriate container, he said, holding out the box. Gucci loafers. Seems nostalgic, now. Oh yeah, and Ed Usher's letter's on a bike. I didn't think your pitch was up enough, so I added some notes.

Penn took the box from him. It had a nice predictable weight to it. Like money. It weighed like a lot of money.

—Thanks, Dean. A guy can always use more Gucci. Ah, wanna come in? Mr Coffee's hot to trot . . .

—Thanks, but I got itchy feet. I'm going to the ocean, smell the surf. Wanna come?

—The ocean? Uh, I guess not. I saw that already. Thanks anyway. Everything okay?

—Okay? You should know, Mance laughed, and Penn heard the change in it right there, a universe away from his habitually cynical, gloating cackle.

—I'll take your word for it, said Penn.

Mance widened his eyes. You mean . . . you never . . . ?

Penn looked at the box in his hands. I'd never have gotten this if I'd seen what you saw.

Mance rubbed the hair on the back of his head thoughtfully. Well, believe me, Cad, you were absolutely right. I didn't lose on this deal. Although really I don't have any idea what the deal was. I'm just glad that it happened. So . . . *glad*. It's like new for me—

—Yeah, sure, right, interrupted Penn, anxious to avoid

hearing another idiot-savant recitative. Have a nice day at the beach.

—Oh, it'll be a little more than a day. I'm backing out of the business for a while. It's just not *me*, you know? You need me, speak to Sandi. Took all night, but I got all the loose ends tied up. Left enough notes to finish Schubert's symphony, poor kid.

Again, Penn was finding the openness of the smile unnerving. He looked down the hall to avoid it, cleared his throat. Yeah . . . take care, Dean. Lay the pipe for me, okay, whatever the surfers do?

Mance tipped him a slow adios-amigo wave, and skipped down the steps, whistling. Penn shut the door and danced cackling into the living room, holding the box aloft like an offering. He knelt and placed it on the table with a ceremonial gesture, lifted the lid, breathing in deeply through his nose.

—I really think, he whispered reverently, the more there is the better it smells. He dug into the thick bundles of hundred-dollar bills, stripped off the paper bands, spilling the notes up in the air, all over the place. Damned if the stuff wasn't giving him a woody. A hundred-thousand-dollar lumber number.

He slipped off his robe, rolled naked on the carpet, grinding his crotch into the cool green windfall, rolled over onto his back and rubbed handfuls of it over his chest, hooting and yodeling. He took a fistful of bills and gripped his pecker in it and worked it up and down quick and firm, and in a voice husky with passion moaned, Ohhhh go-oooooood . . . thank you, god, thank you, thank yooooouuuu . . . woooofffff . . .

SIX

Wax Job in the Comfort Zone

Later, Penn found himself parking at the Z-Mart near
Tuscadero Street because he wanted to check on Tyler
Dupree. The shelf-life of these transformations was important. He'd called Tischia, check her out, got her machine.
Hadn't recognized her at first, a new message in her new
voice, and mumbled something about hoping she was okay,
he'd call later. What if the effect wore off, guys started
putting the bite on him for a refund? He needed to fence
things in with a little paperwork in future, anchor it up.

Dupree seemed more likely to express consumer dissatis-
faction with random bursts of small-arms ordnance than
litigate; still, three hundred and fifty bucks were back-end
points in this deal, and Penn never neglected his back end.
He did a *faux* pimp-roll into the poolroom. Body-language
getting the message across. Yo, I'm hangin' with the homies,
this is my milieu, don' fuck with Cad Penn.

It was a sensory deprivation tank in there. He hooked off
his tortoiseshells, folded them into his jacket pocket, feeling
his fingers trembling. Still couldn't see much, but more than
he wanted. Two pool tables, one ripped up, guys in hooded
sweats watching a kid working on stunt shots. Three guys
huddled up to the bar, laughing, the bartender flicking beer
nuts. He froze in mid-chew, gave Penn a heavy-lidded stare.

One by one everybody in the place stopped talking, turned to look at him. Pool balls stopped clicking, silence thick as a sauna towel. Penn swallowed, feeling like Tipper Gore stumbling onto a Spike Lee set with a tray of Twinkies.

—Uh, hi, he said, in a voice rather higher than he'd have liked. I'm looking for Tyler Dupree? Nobody moved. Penn's back felt like someone was wiping it with a big saltwater fish. Uh, Tyler? he repeated dumbly. Yay big, colored guy . . . uh . . . black . . . shit. His voice cracked. This was not going real well, he told himself. You could be too white. The door creaked open behind him, and he saw his shadow engulfed by another in the flash of sunlight from the street.

—Who wants him, caveboy? Penn recognized the chuckle, and the big hand on his shoulder. Clocked you across the street, Dupree said. Thought I'd swing by and save yo' skinny ass. These mothers never see a white man before.

—Yeah, said the bartender. We gone take yo' picture, stick it on the wall.

Dupree led the way to a table in the corner, called for a couple bags. Torn vinyl kitchen chairs, shadows of the letters on the window slanting BEE on the tabletop, the R curving over Dupree's shoulder.

—Bags? whispered Penn. What do we need bags for?

—Beers, Cad. Don' speak English? Here's yo' three an' a half. Dupree slid a grubby envelope across the table. The smile looked like a permanent fixture on his face.

—Thanks, said Penn, slipping the envelope inside his jacket with a quick look over his shoulder.

—Surprised the nigger kept his word, huh? Fess up.

—Oh, right. I was kind of hoping you'd beat me up again.

—Well, I am myself surprised. In fact, I am in one state of total surprise since I duked you in the gut and I saw . . .

whatever. Also my parole board, and my mother, and the hood rats here hangin' on the bar, they all in one state of surprise that I'm not bustin' folk's asses, that Tyler Dupree's a butter dog all of a damn sudden. Well, I'll be a motherfucker.

—What?

—It really is a Rolex. Dupree held Penn's wrist up, examining the watch.

—My father's. Simple wartime job. Can I ask you a couple questions?

The bartender brought the beers over, staring at Penn. He the cavey?

Penn frowned at Dupree, who nodded, grinning.

—Hey, Joel, said the bartender over his shoulder. Pretty boy here you wanna meet.

—What is this? Penn whispered, the bartender fading into the darkness.

—Tol' my man what happen. He say, s'up, man, what I'm on, I was smiling all the time, not jumpin' on him. Had to tell him something. Science. Can't bullshit no more. Joel here, hey, Joel, siddown. Joel's real fixated on this kind shit.

A lanky guy in a brown satin warm-up jacket with a sleeve fraying off and too-short flannel pants scraped up a chair. May have been about twenty, looked much older on account of his gray frizzed hair, thin nervous-looking face, no teeth. Eyes moving from side to side all the time with the hypnotic rhythm of windshield wipers.

—Wolverines, he said, glancing at Penn.

Dupree chuckled. Homie here tried to get on the Shuggy show with this shit. Has this thing, see, wants to get on the damn show, geek up about wolverines.

—Yeah, said Joel, leaning forward as Penn leaned back.

78

See, wolverine a *mythical* beast. Myth means, fucker don'
exist, nome same?

He looked at Penn as if expecting a response. Penn didn't
feel he had one, made an effort. Well, he said, I guess it's not
hot enough to interest Shuggy. You've got a lot of compe-
tition out there on the Strip.

—Ever clock a wolverine?

Penn smiled in spite of himself. Nope, I guess not.

—No mahfok *ever* clock the wolverine. *Mythical* beast,
like in ancient Rome, unnerstan'. Wolverine *last* mythical
beast.

—They're all dying out? asked Penn ingenuously. Joel's
eye caught his, unnervingly, slid away. Dupree, whose
chuckle had been a quiet accompaniment to Joel's theory,
wiped beer froth off his lip.

—Joel here had other crazy ideas, way back, never got his
ass on the dumb show.

—Jew show, Joel said. Don' see niggers' asses on the
couch.

—Nor many wolverines, said Penn. And Shuggy isn't a
Jew.

—Jew-*ish*, said Joel meaningfully. You got some boom
shit in a fuckin' box, *change* my man, dog look skinnier, pants
hanging off his ass. Shuggy'd be hot for that box . . .

—Whoah, said Penn, holding up a hand and shaking his
head. Time out. Firstly, I don't have anything that did
anything. It's nothing to do with me, right, Tyler?

Dupree thought for a moment. Yeah, you ain't *personal*
responsible for what happen. What is, I don't know. But *you*
ain't.

—Okay, Joel? Second, I have no desire to get on the
Shuggy show. I don't even like the guy.

Joel craned his head around to gawp at Penn. Whaddya mean, you *know* him personal, you don' like him? Or you don' dig the show?

Penn couldn't resist. Even there, even then, even him. Sure, he said, I know the Shugster, on a professional basis. In fact, got a client of mine on just the other night. Maybe you saw her. Tischia Burke White?

—The trick with the drums? said Joel, his hands molding air-breasts.

—Oh shit, said Dupree, you enterin' Joel's wood zone. Dude's carryin' furniture for your trick with the drums. Hey, Joel, wanna leave us alone for a minute? Gentleman wants to ask me some questions.

—You get Joel her name on a drum picture? asked Joel, shuffling away.

—Sure, said Penn, the big star. My pleasure.

—Sorry 'bout that, said Dupree. Joel's, you know, bugged out. You wanna ask me something?

—Yeah. Carrying *furniture* for the trick with the drums?

—Sure. Kind of like a fixture woody he has for your hooter girl. Anything else? Apart from the English class?

—Just touching base here. You still feel the same?

—Uh-huh. Change my mode of existence. Deep.

—So what are you doing? I mean, how has it changed? You quit your dayjob yet?

Dupree chuckled. Could say that. I'm just trying to put shit right. Done a bunch of business. Had to kick that shit to the curb.

—You look good on it.

—In phat shape.

—Well, I don't think so. But you should know what happened to you has happened to others, and it's important to me to know what develops. Keep in touch with any, uh, developments.

—De-*velopments*.

—Yeah. Like, have you noticed anything, like, weird happening?

—As compared to what?

—Well, guy I know claims he can make stones turn into glass, that sort of thing.

—Shit with stones? I guess not, but . . .

—Well?

—Too dumb-ass to mention . . .

—What? What seems too dumb-ass to mention? Mention up, Tyler, it may be important.

—I ain't dissin' you. Like I can hear sunlight?

—Couple days ago, this would have sounded crazy. Not now. Go on.

—It's real quiet, I only get it in the gaps, you know? Like a bunch of notes, violins, classical shit, or humming, when I feel the sun on me. I should go on the Shuggy couch, right? Makes wolverines sound real scientific.

He laughed his deep belly laugh. Penn grinned. Sounds good to me, he said. One other thing. I don't think you should tell anybody else about this. The whole deal. They're going to think you're a nut, and I don't want to be involved, okay? You have my cellphone number, you can call me anytime . . .

—These other dudes you telling me about, that have looked in the box. I'm guessing you ain't one of them, right?

—No.

Dupree finished his beer, belched. You a bigger mystery to me than what I saw in the box, Holmes.

★

Penn didn't see Joel in the car until he slid behind the wheel. Slouched in the passenger seat, cool and bored.

—What the hell? How did you get in here?

—Gettin' in places, Joel's business.

—Yeah? Business get you into Folsom much? C'mon, Joel. Get out my car.

—The fuck you gone do? Call the cops? See any cops round here? He leaned out the window, said, Hey, cops, help. Turned back to Penn and shrugged. Penn looked at him. Skinny but wiry, probably take care of himself. Don't even consider it, mahfok, said Joel, hand sliding into his jacket pocket. Penn sighed.

—What do you want?

—The box, pussy. We cruise to yo' crib and get the fuckin' box, or I smoke yo' ass. You gotta choose the right answer. Like a TV show.

—What *is* it about this neighborhood? said Penn savagely, firing up the ignition. Joel was silent all the way back to Penn's apartment, Penn thinking hard. They bumped into Billy on the landing. Billy stared at Joel with his mouth open, taco chip hanging off his lip. Just showing Joel here the spare room, said Penn breezily. Him and his family looking for a place to live, close to the beach.

—How about under the pier? Billy said. Joel nudged Penn in the hip with something hard and they went inside. Penn wasn't scared, he had a plan. Worked before, it would work again. He went straight to the table with the box on it, thinking, prepare for sainthood, Joel. The tears, the Oscar speech, the subtle lighting effects.

—Freeze yo' ass, fucker, Joel said, kicking the door shut. Penn heard a metallic click, froze his ass.

—Just getting you the box, Joel, he said softly. You

wanted the box, right? His tongue felt like cardboard, and fear was a hard shaming lump in his throat he couldn't swallow. Why him? Joel had no part in this milieu. The guy couldn't even work a fax machine and he was working Penn's life over.

—I clock the fucking box, said Joel. Get yo' ass away from it. Siddown and shut the fuck up.

Penn went where Joel was indicating with the pistol, a blued .38 junkie special, and perched on the BarcaLounger, tipping it forward unsteadily. He didn't know what to do with his hands, for some reason, put them on his knees, under his thighs. Joel was behind him now, and the box was out of reach. Another bad call.

—I thought we were friends, Joel, he said, sounding false and whiny and scared and hating himself. I was going to get you the hooter girl's picture?

—*Fuck* you. This is the fuckin' *Joel* show. Shut yo' fuckin' mout'.

Penn turned his head as Joel's fist whipped across; the room flared in out-of-register negative, and he spun over into himself, slo-mo, fading to black.

SEVEN

My Swine-Flu Hell

—Hey Lyn, said Auburn Cord, fanning her nails dry. You should catch this show, Shuggy Kristiensen? They had Tischia on, and they get all these weirdos from the Strip, not like Tish is a weirdo or anything. Hey! This color is wild! Check it out! Shuggy gets all the crazy guys, and that's why you're here, write about the crazy stuff? Oops, I think I got a little lint on my pinkie nail . . . darn . . . no, it's okay, it blew right off! Can I get you another TriPansodol? You're hurting, huh? Poor baby!

Lyn Crowell struggled out from under the quilt, got up on one elbow and blew her nose on a Kleenex. The couch was strewn with crotted-up tissues, like she was Phlegm Queen in the Pasadena Sickness Parade.

—I feel like shit, she said thickly, horrified at the warm weight of the Kleenex in her hand.

Auburn passed her a silver-blue capsule. Here, take a Tripe, honey, there you go. Hey! They should use that for their ads! Take a Tripe and feel all right . . .

Wearing nothing but nailpolish and foamrubber hair twists, she did a little dance, singing, Got the flu? Here's what you do! Take a Tripe and feel all right! Lyn laughed, finishing with a hacking cough.

Auburn did a cute bow to the applause coming from the

TV, picked up the towel from the floor and wrapped it around her. Onscreen, Shuggy did a little stand-up before unbuttoning his jacket and sliding behind the desk.

—Your typical LA creepfest, said Lyn. He did that button thing guys are always doing.

Shuggy was reading news clippings from cards and mugging reactions to canned laughter.

—Imagine having to go down on that, said Lyn, doing her best not to. Unfortunately, her best was not quite good enough.

—Whaddya think? said Auburn, curled up on the floor, fanning her hands in front of Lyn's face. *I paint my nails . . . ze color of a keeesss . . .*

—*Ravissante*, said Lyn. Hey, check out this bum.

Shuggy was introducing a lanky black guy on the Cuckoo Couch. He held a shoebox on his lap like it contained his science project.

—What he say? said Auburn. He's got no teeth.

—He's got the last mythical beast in the box, apparently. Shuggy's going to get a peep. Here he goes . . .

Shuggy's face is in close-up for the usual mugging reaction shot. Knowing wink to camera just before he looks in the box, conspiratorial yoks from the crew. Cut to two-shot; the black guy holding the box out to Shuggy, peeling back a corner of the lid. The black guy is flinching away. Shuggy appears suddenly very, very anxious. Cut to c/u Shuggy. He looks devastated, like his option has been passed up by the cable station. Then his face softens into a childlike puzzlement, opens into wonder, and his eyes are full of tears. Panstick is running down his cheeks. His mouth works up and down as if he's trying to speak, but there's only a croak. Cut to two-shot; the black guy is gone, the couch is empty.

Shuggy seems transfixed. He pushes a hand up over his face and removes his toupee, placing it carefully on the desk. As he looks to camera a voice-off says, oh, *shiiiit*. Shaky cut to sponsor stab. Dead screen for twenty-three seconds. Wildebeest documentary with voice-over by Tom Bosley.

—Wow, said Lyn. What was *that*?

—Wow, said Auburn. Wow! She thought for a moment, her face puckering prettily. And what is extra *extra* weird, she said, is that you remember I had two broken dates recently? Tish, well, we were going shopping that time to celebrate . . . mm, Spago's! She said something about what her agent had showed her, *in a box*, right? Made *no* sense. And Dean Mance, *ew*, less sleaze, please, he came by to give me that Tiffany pin, that butterfly with the diamonds, and apologize for not taking me out, acting so nice for once, what did he say? Something about a box of tricks? What is it with all these boxes all of a sudden? Is this crazy enough for you or what? Hey, I know this voice . . . this is Tom Bosley? Look at the hairy cows! I met him once. He's a sweetie!

She smiled at Lyn, delighted at all these genuine LA weirdos performing true to type for her friend's benefit.

—Well, I've filled columns with less, said Lyn huskily. Would you mind if I called Tischia, asked her a little more about it?

—Call her machine, you mean. Girl's in a whirl! Sure. If you get through, pass her to me when you're done, huh? She picked the phone off the floor and put it in Lyn's lap, dialing the number for her.

—It's her machine, said Lyn. Hello, Tischia? This is Lyn Crowell, I'm staying with Auburn. I'll call later. It's not important.

—Tol'ja, said Auburn, waving her hands like birds,

86

admiring her shiny nails. Thin air. Like a bird! But to tell the truth, I'm kind of worried?

Lyn blew her nose again, said, Maybe her agent would know? Have you called him?

—Cad? Yeah, we could call him, I guess. Here. She dug for her address book in her purse and dialed, passing Lyn the handset. *Cadogan Penn*, she whispered. Kinda cute. If that's what floats your boat.

—Everyone in LA is somewhere else, Lyn said, hearing Penn's machine kick in. This is Lyn Crowell. I'm a writer, and I'm researching a piece on millennium cults in California, and . . . oh, hello? She heard the clatter of the phone being picked up, and some distant mumbling. Hello? Is that Cadogan Penn?

—What's going on? breathed Auburn, mouthing the words. Lyn waved her quiet, trying to listen.

—Yeah? Did you call the cops?

—Whatwhatwhatwhat? hissed Auburn, her eyes wild and staring.

—A writer, yeah, said Lyn, maybe you saw my piece on the Wilder Cult? It was syndicated . . . oh, okay. Whatever. Sure. I'm staying with Auburn Cord? Tischia's girlfriend? Sure, I can be there. Do you need some help? You sound pretty groggy, you know. Okay. Does Auburn have your address? Lyn saw Auburn nodding vigorously. Great, tomorrow, at ten.

—Nooo! said Auburn, beating her fists on her knees with impatience. I *can't* tomorrow! What is *happening*?

—You were right, Auburn, said Lyn thoughtfully. This *is* weird enough, even for me. This guy Penn? Someone knocks him out in his apartment, steals something. The phone wakes him up. He doesn't want to call the cops for some reason. I'm seeing him tomorrow morning. Let me think this through. Lyn sat up, pushed aside the quilt, frowning. Okay. Couple days ago Penn shows Tischia Burke White something in a box, something that is startling enough to make her break a date with her best friend. That's *you*.

Auburn grinned, fluttering her eyelashes, pleased with her role in the story. Lyn continued. She sounds different on the phone, you said. *Changed*. Okay, but changed. Your word. Next, your date, Dean ants-in-his-pants, drops by to say he *won't* be taking you to the concert, but here's the Tiffany pin like he promised anyway. And something about a box of tricks, which doesn't make sense at the time. And he's changed, too. He wasn't at all what I was expecting from your description.

Lyn took a breath. *Next*, Penn is mugged in his own apartment, something is stolen. He hasn't called the cops. And right there on the television we see Shuggy Kristiensen transformed into a speechless idiot by looking at something in a box held by a shifty-looking guy who then disappears. Is a picture emerging here? Aub?

Auburn was doing ballet movements with her arms. Her towel fell off again. Lyn hated her for her all-over tan, like toasted honey. Auburn said, Shuggy was always an idiot. But I understand your thinking. You're so *cute* at that stuff! But you were the one that went to college, remember. Only book I ever read was *Thirty Days to a Tighter Butt*. It took me that long to finish it! Hahahaha!

Her face creased into seriousness. What's happening, Lyn? Where's Tish? You think she's been got by the goonies or something? You think this is a, a *cult* thing happening?

—Beats me, said Lyn. Mythical beast, the black guy said. What kind of mythical beast do you keep in a shoebox? That makes people crazy when they look at it? All I know is it's a story. And Lyn Crowell, cub reporter, is very definitely on the case. I'm going to soak in the tub. And tomorrow I'm going to be knocking on Cadogan Penn's door an hour early, before the toad gets enough smarts back to cancel.

—And me, said Auburn, stretching like a cat on the pink fluffy towel, I'm going to paint my toenails . . .

—*Ze color of a keeesss*, said Lyn from the door. 'Night, Aub . . .

EIGHT

Holy Cash Cow

The smog lay in a brown fluid toilet stain on the sea's horizon. Just this long, sinister brushstroke, way out there, under a pure blue sky. Lyn stood on the beach and checked the block of duplexes against Auburn Cord's somewhat fuzzy description. A fat woman in a pink jogging suit was using a pooperscooper at the bottom of the steps. Lyn waited for her to finish, thinking, I bet she worries about salt in her diet, too. This dietary faddishness was fantastic to Lyn, coupled with the fact that they were poisoning their blood-stream with every breath. The fat woman jogged off, poodle tippy-tapping at her heels.

Lyn checked her look in the mirrorglass door. Foxy yet professional, she told herself, if younger than her twenty-five years. Thankfully, Auburn's skill with the Leichner brush had virtually eliminated Kleenex chafe. She wore loose-cut brown Levis, a short-sleeve beige linen blouse with gold coin buttons, gold earrings, rope sandals with gold fasteners. She carried a slim Coach pocketbook and her sunglasses. Her jet-black hair fell short of her shoulders in a straight bob, and her nails were painted *ze color of a keeesss*. Auburn had done that for her too.

She opened the door and went up the steps. A guy stood on the landing wearing an outsize foam stetson with an arrow through it, *Baywatch* boxer shorts and cartoon animal slippers which squeaked as he shifted his weight. He whistled at her through his teeth. A real old-fashioned pre-PC wolf-whistle.

—Cadogan Penn? she said, grimacing.

—Sure, why not? Naah, I wish, he leered. He pointed down the hall with his chin. Next apartment, doll-face. I hope you get the spare room. Come see mine if you don't like his. Mine is, uh, bigger. *If* you know what I mean.

Lyn frowned at him and walked down the hall, feeling his eyes on her. She stopped, and without turning said, and *I* hope you have the longest dick in the world.

—Yeah? he said dumbly, letting her know he was eyeing her up.

—That way, said Lyn, when I tell you to go fuck yourself I won't be wasting my breath. *If* you know what I mean, dog-face.

She heard another whistle, smiled grimly, and pressed the buzzer above the little window with Penn's name written on a scrap of paper behind it. The door was opened by a man holding a plastic sack of frozen French beans against the side of his head.

—Oh, hi, he said. Actually, I called to cancel . . .

—But I'm here already, Lyn grinned. Well, can I come in?

—Uh . . . I guess . . .

She followed him into the living room. He just stood holding the bag to his head, not speaking, not looking anywhere in particular. He was wearing a crumpled dark cotton suit with no shoes, had bags under his eyes, and looked like Lyn felt, which was still shit, in spite of necking back three TriPansodol with her five-fruit juice.

—Coffee? he said quietly. It's decaff. I just made a fresh pot. Excuse me. It hasn't been a great night. Sit down, please . . .

—I'd love a coffee.

He left her to check out all the predictable bachelor styling touches: the graphic colors, the metal, the black boxes with the little lights.

—So, he called from the kitchenette. Why don't you tell me why you're here? I wasn't too clear last night, I'm afraid. You're a writer?

He brought the coffees through and sat down opposite, putting the black Apilco cups on the table.

—Well, a journalist, if that counts, said Lyn, taking a sip of coffee. I'm staying with an old girlfriend of mine, Auburn Cord? She and I were at school together. Anyway, I'm researching a piece on cults here in LA, you know, religious sects vibing up for the millennium, what they see happening.

—Yeah, okay, but how can I help? I don't get the connection. Penn groaned, touched his head. Lyn saw the bruise on his temple and a long, scabbed-over graze on his cheek.

—Ouch, she said, wincing in sympathy. You should get that looked at.

—It's okay. Just left me a little dazed.

—You got mugged in your own apartment? What do you do, invite them up? She watched him take a sip of coffee. A good-looking guy, in a lazy kind of way. A little too spoilt-looking for her tastes. Easy life, probably, old money, with a name like that.

—I guess, he said. So, back to you. I'm afraid you're following a cold lead here. But go ahead.

She felt a sneeze building up, panicked for a Kleenex in her pocketbook, caught it just in time.

—*Gesundheit!* said Penn.

—Thank you, Lyn sniffled. Look at me. What a mess. Excuse me.

—You look just fine, said Penn, his eyes making brief contact with hers.

—Okay, Lyn said, tucking the Kleenex back in her bag. To business. Did you catch the Shuggy Kristiensen show last night? No, of course you didn't. You were sleeping like a baby.

—Ah, I don't get it. Your point being? Can we stop being so damned elliptical?

—Let me tell you something about the guy who mugged you, Lyn said, leaning forward to put her coffee on the table. Black, kind of lanky, wearing a brown jacket with a torn sleeve? She watched, with some satisfaction, as his eyes got bigger. She had him.

—Oh no, he said in a pained voice. You're a cop.

She shook her head. God no! I look like a cop? But I understand why you couldn't call them last night. Kind of hard to explain what he stole, isn't it? She watched him as he finished the coffee, using the time to think up a response.

—If I may repeat myself, Miss, er, Crowell, could you please just tell me why you're here? I have had possibly the worst night of my life, and a really cramped day ahead. Core this out for me.

—I'm interested in the box you had. I'm interested in the effect it's having on people. People like Tischia Burke White, Dean Mann . . .

—Mance, interrupted Penn, thinking, whoops.

—And Shuggy Kristiensen. At this, Penn sat upright, forgetting all attempts at dissembling. He repeated the name in disbelief. The man himself, nodded Lyn. Shame you didn't manage to crawl to the VCR before blacking out.

Penn snapped his fingers. Wait here, he said. While he was gone Lyn looked the room over again. Toy car. Pictures of cars. Stroke magazine on the floor. This was the room of a big kid. The big kid came back waving a cassette.

—My neighbor may still eat by surrounding things with his butt, but he has his uses. He collects cable talk-shows. Women Who Marry Their Morticians and the Husbands Who Want Them to, that kind of deal. He has an entire wall full of the stuff, date order, cross-referenced.

—My! He's a real catch.

Penn was down on his knees, fumbling with the VCR. Nice buns, thought Lyn. Penn rocked back on his heels and pointed the remote. They watched the tape in silence. Penn spooled through the transformation scene three times, and left it in freeze-frame, just where Shuggy pushes off his toupee.

—Shit, he said eventually, slumping back into the couch and running his hand back through his hair. Holy fucking excuse me shit.

He looked so bleak, yet Lyn found it impossible to feel sorry for the guy. Something to do with a little tap on the head constituting the worst night of his life. Poor *baby*.

—So, she said. Want to talk?

Penn got up slowly, face in his hands, went to the window. It's over, he said. Whatever you're looking for, it's gone. I lost my girl, my business, and that's just the start of what I don't have anymore. All I have is a cluster migraine and stomach cramps. Is that news?

94

—Depends if it's your period. Look at this from my perspective. I'm following up a story here. It may not be exactly the one I drove all the way from Utah to get, but it's still *a* story. Either you work with me or you don't. If you work with me, I get a better story. I'm not looking at you as an enemy, so you come across better. And, who knows, maybe you'll get your mythical beast back.

She saw Penn turn from the window, raise his head, and start in astonishment, staring at something behind her. What the *fuck*?

Lyn swiveled in the chair. Standing in the open doorway was a tall figure dressed in a home-made satin superhero costume, brown leotard with a green W on the chest, brown fur cape, and a ratty-looking fur animal mask. Under one arm was a shoebox, the other raised in a heroic gesture.

—I am . . . the Wolverine!

Penn burst out laughing, stopped himself. The Wolverine moved silently to the table and put the box on it. The Wolverine's mission, he said in a familiar gummy voice, protec' the 'merican way of life an' return stolen shit to their rightful owners, nome same? You wanna grab the Wolverine, leave a message at the pool hall on Tuscadero.

He swirled his cape around and sprang for the door. When he'd gone, Penn rushed to the table and put his hands on the box, as if feeling for a heartbeat. He was laughing, but Lyn didn't find the tone attractive.

—Mysterious ways, Penn chuckled. Come to Dada. Well, Miss Crowell, I guess you can add someone else to the list of people who've looked in the box.

—How did *he* get in? she said, looking from the door to Penn in disbelief. Did you leave the door open? And who the hell *was* it?

—The Wolverine, Penn said solemnly. I can only tell you locked doors mean *nothing* to this guy.

—Oka-ay, she said, hunting for her recorder amongst the Kleenex harvest in her pocketbook. I think I could make a wild guess, anyway. Why don't we start with how you came by the box? This *is* the box, I take it? I'm just switching this doohickey on now, we're rolling. Go ahead.

—What, now? said Penn stupidly.

—Sure. No time like the present. Leaving aside the question of what's inside for a moment . . . where did you get it?

Penn went to the window again, clutching the box to his chest, stroking it with his fingers. It gave Lyn the creeps. I got to get some more ice, he said.

She gave him a wry look and switched off the tape while he rummaged in the icebox in the kitchenette, came out clasping a bag to his head, the box still under his arm. He nodded. She switched the tape back on.

—I found it, he said firmly. Outside a shoe store.

—In the trash? So how did you know there was something special about it? It looks like an ordinary shoebox with the brand name on it, Ampar? And a picture of a shoe. So? I mean, why pick it up?

—I don't know. I thought there might be some shoes in it.

—You don't know. You thought there might be some shoes in it. And you looked inside?

—No.

—Why not?

—I was being mugged.

—What? Is this something you make a habit of?

—Believe me, not until recently. The guy kicked the shit

out of me, took the box and looked into it. I saw what happened to him, put the lid right back. Listen, can we do this some other time?

—You were mugged for some shoes you'd just found in the trash. This guy, is he our friend the Wolverine by any chance?

—No, this is another guy. Tyler Dupree. We're big buddies. We *vibin'*. An' shit. Hangs out on Tuscadero Street. The Tusc.

—Home of the Wolverine.

—Same locale. Want some more coffee?

—No thanks. So how did Tischia Burke White come to look in the box?

—I'm her agent. Was her agent. She was being difficult. A pain in the ass like you wouldn't believe. After I saw this box deal turn Dupree into Pat Boone, I figured it might soften her up a little. *Big* surprise. Excuse me, there's my phone.

Penn put the box on the table, giving her a look, and went to the telephone table at the end of the couch to take the call, standing with his back to her. She looked at the box, uncomfortably tempted to take a peek. She could just reach out, flip the lid off, find out what was really at the heart of this stupid story. If there *was* anything. Penn turned to grin at her, replacing the phone.

—Wanna see a man make a million dollars?

—I guess the answer to that should be probably not. One more question. It's important. Now you know what the box does, don't you want to let it do its stuff on you? Looks like you could use a little healing.

Penn picked up the box in both hands, tilting it from side to side. Nope, he said thoughtfully, I'd rather make a little

97

money out of the sucker first. What with the rent due. How about you? Come on. I know you were tempted just now. It's only natural. Wanna take a peek?

Lyn looked at the box, sucking her lip. She looked at Penn. Call the bastard's bluff, she thought. Yeah, she said slowly. It would certainly help with my story. Provide valuable first-hand experience. Okay. Yes. I will look in your shoebox.

Penn offered her the box and, as Lyn put a hesitant hand out to touch it, he drew it back out of reach.

—Well, Miss Crowell, you can't, he said in a nyah-nyah-nyah voice. And you can't, simply because you can't *afford* it. From now on, god is for the rich. Goodbye Compton, hello Beverly Hills. Tough break, huh? Especially after all these criminal types been getting their jollies for free. But hey, we can't keep the man with the million waiting. Ready?

In the car, with the box in a locked aluminum photographer's case on the back seat, Lyn listened to Penn telling her how he got where he was today. She hadn't asked to hear it, and it wasn't particularly interesting. He had this image of himself as a Hollywood player, which was almost naive enough to be touching, but was finally insulting because he considered her naive enough to believe it.

She kept asking what it was he actually *did*, and he kept avoiding a clear answer. Maybe, she reflected, this was how things were in 'this town'. Maybe there was a whole stratum of LA society that couldn't answer that question. Not because they had anything to hide, but because they didn't actually *do* anything in the rest-of-the-world sense.

She got the very strong impression that Cadogan Penn

couldn't actually do anything. Anything like change a tire. Recognize major food groups. Perform open-heart surgery. Play a musical instrument. Name a tree. Toss a shrimp salad. Maybe he could toss a shrimp salad. Only in LA would a guy like this stand a chance, and even here he'd needed what she guessed to be quite a sizable fund from a dead relative to last this long. Back in Utah he'd be bear breakfast, day one.

They drove up into Beverly Hills, and Lyn was surprised by how *green* it was. And, well, how *nice* it was. She'd expected pink plastic Barbie houses patrolled by Nixon-era Whitehouse stormtroopers, and said so.

—Yeah? said Penn. You don't know this town too well. How are you liking it?

—LA? Where *is* it? I've been driving around for days and I never found it.

—What, you want a little town square with a schoolroom and a courthouse and a barbershop? I think they have a couple out at Disneyland.

—*Exactly*. Plastic.

—Wow, what an insightful critique. I never heard that before. Your fresh innocent worldview has left me momentarily stunned by its childlike acuity.

—You know what I mean. It's like the whole place was made up by someone who was never here.

They pulled into a driveway entrance framed by manicured yews.

—Well, I hope you can connect with the reality of this, Penn said. This is real estate. You're looking at Ed Usher's retirement plan, and today he's going to turn it over to me. Did I say a million bucks? I was *hopelessly* off track. No wonder Dean didn't think my pitch was up enough.

He spoke into a silver grille set in a brick gatepost. Lyn

couldn't help gawping. The gates were black wrought iron, with gilt metal ivy curling around *Arkady* in green enamel script. Each gate probably cost more than her apartment back in St George, and was substantially larger. They put her life in some sort of perspective. The kind of perspective you see in German expressionist movies. The gates swung open silently, and they drove up through mature elm, oak, hornbeam . . . She stopped naming trees and felt a sudden twinge of apprehension.

—Uhh, Mr Penn . . .

—Call me Cad.

—Whatever. Listen, I don't know what you're planning here exactly, but I don't want to be party to anything, you know, of dubious legality.

Penn laughed. Dubious legality? What's that? Anyway, it's a little late to ankle back to Utah, isn't it? Hey, check this out. Now this is *really* real estate. Really *really* real.

Ed Usher's mansion was solid English tudorbethan, with fired-earth tiled roofs sweeping down around twisty fairytale chimneys. Black oak half-timbered brick walls, mullioned windows, leaded lights, and ivy everywhere. The grass looked like a mechanically tinted picture in a vacation brochure, super-saturated green. Lawn sprinklers carelessly tossed lazy loops of diamonds into the air. They swept past a five-car garage, Lyn catching a gleam of gunmetal paintwork in the shade, and pulled up by the golden stone steps leading up to the massive front door. Someone in a white major-domo jacket came down the steps and opened her door. Penn had to open his own door.

—Welcome to Arkady, the man said, in an English accent. Mr Usher is expecting you. Everyone is at the pool. Will you follow me?

100

Penn took the camera case from the back seat and did his jacket up.

—Why do you do that? Lyn whispered, as they passed through an entrance lobby like a medieval church stuffed with tapestries and suits of armor.

—Do what? said Penn.

—That *button* thing . . . Oh, never mind. Penn frowned at her. Well, she thought, men were always doing up or undoing their jackets and she couldn't see the logic. Another time maybe. She took off her sunglasses and slipped them into her pocketbook. More than anything else right now she wanted to blow her goddam nose. They walked into what appeared to be an exhibition of Nazi war loot in a tastefully converted baseball stadium. It was a little like those Tom and Jerry cartoons, she reflected, where you see the same table and chair go by on an endless wall. Islands of chintz and gold and mahogany furniture. Strangely familiar oil paintings. Scarily muscular floral displays that sucked the air right out of your lungs.

—I feel like Alice, you know? she snuffled. When she gets real tiny?

—Here, said Penn a little irritably, passing her a handkerchief. It was Irish linen, freshly laundered. She blew her nose extravagantly, went to pass it back. He waved it away.

—Thanks, she said, more genuinely grateful than he'd ever know. She pushed it into the pocket of her Levis. They were now in a conservatory big enough to qualify as an emergent nation. One side opened out onto a Yorkstone patio surrounding the pool, and beyond that a lawn greener than money. The grounds were so big you could see the back of your own head in the distance. Bodies lay on wheeled recliners in the luminous shade of white umbrellas, like they were waiting for the *ER* team to straddle them with booster cables. A bald man with a neat gray mustache slid a copy of *Variety* off his stomach and got up to greet them. He wore a pale blue short-sleeve shirt and madras shorts.

—Cad, he said, a smile creasing his tan face. Good to see you.

He turned his smile to Lyn. Penn shook his hand and made the introduction. Lyn Crowell, Ed Usher. Lyn's a writer. I'm, uh, showing her around.

—Lyn, how are you? Who are you with?

She took his hand. Oh, you know, she heard herself say. An attempt to be casual that made her grate her teeth. She could almost hear Penn thinking, well, *Utah*, what can you expect.

—Uh-huh, Usher said. So, Cad. You have something mysterious and wonderful to show me, I understand? I hope it's germane to Dean's disappearance. Although no-one is irreplaceable, everyone has their place, right? He switched his gaze back to Lyn. If you'll excuse us? He turned to the group under the umbrellas. Everybody? Cad here and I are going into the house for twenty minutes. Say hello to Lyn. Simon? Where's . . . oh, Simon, will you fix Lyn a drink?

The people on the loungers smiled glassily and nodded at her, flopped back into torpor. The man in the white jacket appeared at her elbow and asked what she'd like to drink. Lyn asked if she might have a cup of Earl Grey and he glided off.

—English, said a big pink Jewish-looking man, wagging a porky forefinger at Simon's retreating back.

—I'm sorry? said Lyn.

—They do that servile schtick like no-one else on the planet, believe you me. Going for a swim?

—Uh, I guess not, I have this damn flu?

—Yeah? Whole town coming down with it. What are you taking? He rotated his head on his fat neck and spoke loudly to a woman behind him. She wore a pink frilled swimsuit and a towel over her head and her legs were propped open with a Thighmaster. He had an increasingly irritable conversation with her, trying to remember pharmaceutical brand names, her voice virtually inaudible through the towel. Lyn left them to it and wandered off to look at the pool. It was circular, with small glinting tiles in shades of inky blue, and empty except for a translucent green inflatable dinosaur at its center, as motionless as if it were set in crystal. She looked at the inert bodies under the umbrellas. The arguing couple had shut up. Everything was bright and airless and hard and completely still. There was a head-bursting sense of something about to happen, of time about to keel over, like a toy top losing its spin. Could she be the only one to feel it? The silence banged like a big dumb iron bell in her head.

—Your tea, madam. She involuntarily put her hand to her heart, gasped. I'm sorry, Simon said, I startled you. Will you take it in the shade? You'll get a nasty headache out here.

Simon had just got Lyn settled in the welcome cool of a vine-hung loggia when Penn bounded out of the conservatory doors, did a kind of pirouette with his hands stuck in his pant pockets, spotted her, clicked a finger-pistol, and skipped over. His grin was as broad as an ad. He bent forward theatrically, from the waist.

—Say hello to the new owner!

—What?

—His lawyers are swinging by to anchor it up this pm. A formality. Penn spread his arms and did another twirl, his head thrown back. All mine! he cried. Now he had the attention of the people on the loungers, who raised their heads and visored up their sunglasses to look at him. He was hooting and barking with laughter, stamping his feet in a kind of spastic Indian dance, singing mine-mine-mine, miney-miney-miney-mine. Now he was writhing on the ground, moaning and kissing and actually *licking* the stones.

—Penn, for god's *sake*! snapped Lyn, getting to her feet, but it was no good. He'd hopped over to the guests and was prodding them in the stomach, cackling, throwing paperbacks into the pool. Lyn, furious and embarrassed, strode into the house, straight through the conservatory into the living room, where she circled desperately, clutching the handkerchief to her face.

—Come sit down, said a kindly voice. Please. Sit down. Take it easy.

She stopped in her tracks, saw Ed Usher waving at a chintz armchair next to the one he sat in. He was smiling.

—God, she said, I am so sorry, Mr Usher, I, I . . .

—Hey hey hey. Sit with me. You're sick.

She sat down, looking warily at Usher. Something about his eyes.

—Listen, I'm not with him. I hardly know him. He's crazy, right?

Usher laughed softly. Like a fox, as they say.

Lyn turned away from him to blow her nose. When she looked back she saw his eyes, unblinking, smiling, and something else going on there. Something weird. She said, But he's yelling about being the new owner . . . there, you can hear him. There was a splash from the pool, voices raised in anger.

—Oh, said Usher. But he is. There's a little paperwork to

be done, but that's more to reassure him than anything else. In my heart, Arkady is his, and everything in it. And he's welcome to it.

—Did you see in the box? Lyn asked thickly.

The voices were getting closer, and Lyn heard Penn's hyena laugh. Usher leaned forward and patted her knee. Why don't we go somewhere quiet? He stood up, took her hand, and led her to a small paneled room off the main hall, lined with books. She sat in a green leather club chair and Usher perched close by on the edge of a walnut writing desk.

—In answer to your question, he said, yes, I saw in the box. And I am more than pleased to hold up my end of the bargain. More than pleased. *Therefore* – he waved a hand – the new owner. This is entirely my own decision, you have to understand. There was no coercion, and I'm keeping to my word.

The voices in the hallway retreated into the distance. They could hear cursing, a woman crying hysterically, and hoots of insane laughter.

—Back in the old days, continued Usher, you had to keep to your word, it was all you had. Now we got attorneys to keep it for us, tell us what it is if we forget. And we do forget, because they keep changing it. This deal was a good old-fashioned piece of business, and the best handshake I ever made. Period.

—But why? What could you possibly have seen that makes you want to give all this away? I don't get it. This is a lifetime's hard work here, and you're giving it to someone for a peek in a shoebox? A trick peepshow? Are you *kidding*?

—Lyn, I'm aware here that you're focusing on the shoebox, or Cad Penn maybe, but these things are peripherals.

They're not what the deal is about. I'm not a writer. I don't have your skill for, you know, making things vivid through words. With that in mind, let me try anyway. If I say I saw god, I'm using, what, a metaphor? In the sense that I didn't see a picture of god, like Charlton Heston. If I say there was a bright light, but no source to it, no lightbulb, it sounds like new-age baloney. It was both those things, and neither. It was more something I felt, to be honest. Something I still feel. *Alive*. But there's this, I don't know, moral quality to it? Like there's no distinction between alive and good. And I can tell you that this house, which I built for my late wife, god rest her soul, this house just seems suddenly . . . *empty*. An empty box of bricks and wood. The guy's welcome to it, if that's what he wants, emptiness. That's the closest I'm going to get here. I've *got* what's in the box. I *am* what's in the box. I don't need the box it came in. Ah, this isn't helping you any, is it?

Lyn stretched up toward him, narrowing her eyes. Would you mind, she said, if I looked . . . lean down a little here, turn your head, in your eyes . . .

There was something moving in his eyes, colors and shapes flicking across the iris.

—What do you see? said Usher.

—Um, it's like pictures? Tiny, tiny movies, playing in your eyes. I thought it was reflections, but it's not. It's . . . beautiful.

Usher laughed. Is my name in the credits? Who's featuring?

—Too tiny to tell.

—Well, he said. I better go clear things up with my guests. They're not going to take Cad's word for it, that's for sure.

—No, no-one would. Lots of luck.

She sat and stared at the fresh-cut flowers in the fireplace after he'd gone, listening to doors slamming, voices shouting, and tires spitting gravel in the driveway. Eventually Penn put his head round the door. He looked flushed, and his hair was all over the place. His necktie had been wrenched over his shoulder, and the sleeve of his jacket was soaked.

—Hey, you're here, he said.

—Right. Great.

He pushed his fingers through his hair. Guess I went a bit wild out there, huh?

—You lost it.

—Yeah . . .

—Big time.

He came in and tapped the back of her chair with his fingers. You're right. Absolutely right. I guess I got overexcited. Well, excuse me. It's the first time anyone gave me some billion-dollar real estate. You, you can afford to be blasé, right? Miss Frosty-cool here.

Lyn found her sunglasses in her bag and put them on. Her hands were trembling. She felt confused and hot and sick. Was all this craziness just swine-flu brain fever?

—I'm not up for this right now, she said. Whatever it is, whoever you are. She swayed out into the hall, where Simon took her arm.

—Mr Usher has asked LeVar to drive you home, if you're ready? He helped her down the steps to where a liveried driver held open the door of a gunmetal Lexus.

—You know what? Penn shouted after her from the steps as she slid into the back seat. You want a story? Let me tell you something. I'll tell you something. *This* is the greatest story ever fucking told, and you're just walking away. Just walking away!

He was miming walking with his fingers, repeating *just walking away* in a sing-song voice as they drove off. Obnoxious, irritating and just plain wrong right to the last, Lyn thought.

She let herself into Auburn's apartment and saw the note right away, propped up against the Garfield clock on the TV.

Lyn, it read, *something fantastic has happened Tish is back!!!!! its sooo exciting I'll call later in the week maybe to explain don't worry stay as long as you need!!!!!!! DON'T WORRY!!!!!!! ps the chili is defrosting luv AUB XXXX*

There was a big smudged lipstick kiss at the bottom. She frowned at the note for quite a long time, between sneezes. Not even the chili part made any sense. Nothing made any sense. She stumbled out of her clothes and dove into bed, a long long way away down a hot, sweaty, aching tunnel.

When she clawed her way back into consciousness she was only dimly aware it was morning. Which morning, she had no idea. Sunlight glowed through the muslin rollerblind, blurred shadow of a palmleaf falling across it. She got up, feeling like the fever had passed, went to the bathroom, took a shit and a shower and washed her hair. Auburn's apartment was strangely quiet, no solid gold seventies music on the radio. Another mystery disappearance. Another mystery. She focused on the routine to prevent the craziness of the previous day immobilizing her. Every time she found herself thinking something impossible she gave herself something reasonable to do, to get her head clear. Fix breakfast. Make the bed. Rinse the tub. She loaded the washing machine, sidetracked momentarily by the initials on the handkerchief,

CP. Made pancakes for brunch. All this homely chore stuff wasn't helping, and she knew it. She dialed Penn's cellphone number. She heard his voice before it even rang.

—What.

—Penn?

—What?

—This is Lyn. Where are you?

—At home. Remember?

—Listen, Aub's gone. She may be with Tischia Burke White.

—So?

—So, it's another disappearance. Everyone around you is taking a hike out of their lives.

—Your point being?

—You're the most annoying man I ever met. The point being that you should know that I'm onto you. This whole thing is some kind of cheap scam and you're the cheapie scamming it. I don't believe your story. Of course I don't believe it. In fact, as *policy*, I don't believe anything you say. I think you're a crook, and I think you're extorting people, that's what I think. You want my perspective? I'm going to blow the lid right off this thing.

—Oh, very good. *Blow the lid off.* I'm so-oo scared. But this is a little insulting, you know. I hate you thinking there's anything cheap about me, I hate it. Tell you what; you have my absolute permission to take a meeting with any of my clients, and get their own perspective. Which has more relevance than yours, I think.

—Your *clients*?

—I believe you'll find Tyler and Joel at the poolroom, a block east of the Porn Baron on Tuscadero, if you feel like slumming down. You're Woodward and Bernstein here, you know who my clients are, you find them. But you'll be wasting your time.

—How so?

—The real story's here with me. Aren't you excited?

—I'm irritated. Clients, my ass.

—You're eating something. What are you eating?

—Pancakes.

—Wow. Come bake me some pancakes.

—Staff problems?

—No staff, no problems.

—No pancakes.

—I'll pick you up at eight.

Lyn powered up her laptop, gritting her teeth. Cadogan annoying-son-of-a-bitch Penn. For a writer, she thought, she was doing precious little of it.

Lyn liked Tyler Dupree. She felt safe with him, like he was this big calming protective presence. But the fact that he backed up Penn's story didn't make her like Penn any, and his transparent honesty only made Penn's glib half-truths flimsier by comparison. Penn's story, she thought, stank worse than the poolroom bar they sat in, sinking cold Buds while Dupree patiently answered her questions, went through it all again. Lyn was surprised to learn that he'd mugged Penn right there, twenty yards up the street. She'd assumed that Dupree had bussed to work, get better clients. What would a nice 'burb-wasp like Penn be doing here, rooting through the Tuscadero trash? The shoe stores were full of inflatable glow-in-the-dark stink-foot penitentiary pumps, and Penn was strictly loaded for Lobb. So his story right up to Dupree's appearance was a crock of shit without the crock to hold it. She asked Dupree if he had any idea.

—Maybe looking for his radio. Lifted that the day before, couple days, I forget. He got it back. Still working on the other shit.

Lyn frowned. He was here *before*? Why?

—Visiting with some punk used to rent over the porno store. Caveboy with green hair.

—Green hair? That doesn't sound like Penn's tennis crowd to me. Was he down here buying drugs?

—Could be. You can buy every kind shit here, you got the connection. Every jones catered for. That punk was into all kinds shit. Ain't there no more. All his shit out in the street.

Lyn told him about the Wolverine's appearance at Penn's apartment. Dupree shook with laughter, his belly up against the table making the bottles rattle. You dig the dog's flava? he giggled. My mom make him the suit, use a bunch of stupid shit for that.

—Very impressive. How do I reach him?

Tyler tapped the side of his nose and winked. Like this, he whispered, and, throwing his head back, uttered a long, high wolf-call. A second later the Wolverine appeared out of the darkness at the back of the bar, yawning.

—Yo. Who call the Wolverine from his lair of solitude?

—He sleep back there in the daytime, Tyler said in an aside to Lyn. Join us here, Joel. Lady wants to ask you some questions.

The Wolverine swept his threadbare cloak aside with a flourish and sat down. I met this lady already. Cad Penn's hottie. He's one lucky white nigger.

Lyn denied being anyone's *hottie* and told him what she was doing, why she was there, and asked what had happened on the Shuggy show.

111

—You dug that, huh. Bloods clockin' the Shuggy show that time. Joel ran his ass out of there, Shuggy poppin' weird faces an' shit, thought my man's about to ice up on me. Mos' blunt experience. Joel run home like a motherfucker, fell right up the step, box opens up, shit, face stuck right in it. Had to pull it off of my head, see?

He mimed pulling the box off his face.

—So you didn't intend to look in it? asked Lyn.

The Wolverine shook his head vigorously. Wanted to work Shuggy over first, check it out. After *his* face, no *way* Joel peek in there. Weird shit in that box.

—So what did you see?

The Wolverine shrugged. Same as Tyler, I guess. Don't recollect.

—Was it a mythical beast, like you said on the show?

—Wasn't nothin'. It was bright. Real quick, like nothin' happened. Like a kid again, yeh. Real rush feeling. *Boom* shit!

—Was it like a drug rush? Like doing crack or something?

The Wolverine gave her a gummy smile. Ain't never done shit like that. Trashed my lungs on schwag bud. And Joel done a assload of party shit. No way I touch that shit ever again in my life, Tyler neither, right, Ty?

He put his head on one side, listening. Lyn went to say something, but Dupree put a finger to his lips. Somebody needs the Wolverine, man, he's out of here.

The Wolverine leaped to his feet, knocking his chair over, and charged outside.

—Wanna take a look? asked Dupree.

—Does a wolverine shit in the woods?

Outside, a small crowd had gathered at the corner, pointing up. There was a four-story bricked-up warehouse at the intersection, blackened with fire damage. A broken sign on the edge of the roof, AMERICAN PARADI in big flaking letters on a buckled framework. Someone had climbed to the top of the sign and was trying to stand up. He wore orange-colored pants and an undershirt. People were yelling, Jump, motherfucker, jump, you stupid fuck. The guy sat on top of the C and kicked his house-slippers off, screamed something.

Lyn saw the Wolverine elbowing into the crowd, getting pushed back. She looked up just in time to see the guy jump and drop into the scattering crowd, arms pumping comically, turning over slowly as he fell. His head hit the sidewalk first and burst like a grape. The crowd whooped with disgusted laughter. Lyn clamped her hand to her mouth, feeling sick. Dupree put his hand on her shoulder, turned her away.

—Not even the Wolverine could have caught that one, he said.

—Those sick bastards. They were urging him to do that.

She unlocked her Pinto and got inside. She felt sweaty and nauseous. Dupree bent down to speak to her, and she noticed he wasn't smiling anymore.

—Well, he said, tell you something. Before I saw in that box, whatever it was, I'd be in there yelling the loudest. Sickest motherfucker on the street. 'Cept maybe for Joel. He'd of been up there on the roof giving the guy a push. Joel was always a nut, but now, you understan', he's trying to do the right thing down here. That's all we're trying to do. Something right. Dupree's grin returned. Say hello to Ralph Lauren for me.

She drove past the Porn Baron store, the perverts out blinking in the sunshine, eyeing the drama down the street. Another time, she thought, her lip curling disgustedly. The punk's trail would just have to get a little colder. A siren blipped loudly, and the green lawns of Arkady seemed like a very long way away. Somewhere in the back of her mind something was bothering her. She rewound the tape, cued it forward until she found it. There it was. The Wolverine's gummy mumble. *Face stuck right in it. Had to pull it off of my head, see?*

This was an empty box they were talking about.

NINE

A Swank Necktie by Day, a Glowing Call to Love by Night

The Lexus drifted up into the hills. Lyn looked out over the city, flickering like a badly tuned TV in the haze-filtered twilight. The twin crystal clusters of downtown and Century City, erupting from the flat mineral silt of LA. It was appropriate, she thought, that such a self-obsessed place should wrap itself in a reflective blanket of its own waste.

—Beautiful, yeah? said Penn, slowing so she could take it in.

—Well, big, anyway, she said. So many people.

—Yeah. And it's a sobering thought that, even as we speak, a statistically significant proportion of them are introducing barnyard animals into their sphincters.

Penn grinned as he saw her avoid giving him the pleasure of a reaction. Lyn concentrated on gazing out at the skyline. The cheap cocktail spark of an LA sunset held no romance for her. She was being driven to a billionaire's mansion in Beverly Hills by a handsome, rich, unmarried, heterosexual male, and what she felt was mostly irritation.

She'd thrown off the fever, and the better she felt the more annoyed she got. Annoyed with Cadogan Penn for all kinds of reasons, and furious with herself for not being able to see through what was happening. Reason dictated the whole thing was a put-on, but her meetings with Usher, Tyler and the Wolverine didn't fit the pattern. A scam needed dupes. They didn't seem like dupes to her. They seemed like the most straight, honest, clear people she'd ever met. Even Joel, in his way. And where was Penn's percentage in involving Tuscadero Street at all? Why bother? What was Penn saying?

—He-llo? he said musically, twisting his face around in front of hers at an intersection.

Lyn started. Uh, sorry, swine-flu flashback . . . You were saying?

—I was *saying* that Usher's giant snapping turtle lawyers were just over, and, boy, were they pissed. Old Ed just sat there saying it was already history, he'd given me the house and everything in it and that was the deal, and he was happy with it. His lawyers reckon the estate will sue him, sue me, get the decision reversed in the courts. Oh yeah, and the IRS is going to be down my throat with wirecutters, apparently.

—You don't sound concerned.

—What, me worry? Fuck 'em. I got god in a box. I got the whole wo-orld, in my hands . . .

Lyn remembered Joel, face stuck in the box. The empty box. Tell me, she said. This box. What does it feel like? Is it heavy? I mean, what does god *weigh*?

—A probing question from the lady in the fetching lavender ensemble. Since you ask, nothing. There's a strange shifting feel to it sometimes, when you move it, but it feels like it's empty, in terms of weight. I'll let you hold it if you're good.

She gave him a sidelong glance. What was it about him,

116

she didn't believe *anything* he said? Even when, like just now, he seemed to be telling the truth? It was like he spoke both truths and untruths with the same superficial topnotes of an acquired *sincerity*; as if he didn't, or couldn't, make the distinction. So everything he said was filtered through this delusional gauze. Did he think she took him at his word? Did he think she was that stupid? Did he think at all? Cadogan Penn had a big problem with truth and honesty, she decided.

—So, she said, you got your house in the hills, you got your oil paintings and your big limo ... your *empty* shoebox ...

—*And* a '66 wire-wheel Jaguar E-Type with showroom mileage ...

—And your musical Elvis Poptart Kiln. So I don't expect you'll be hangin' with the homies from the 'hood no more, is what I'm sayin', dig?

—I rather doubt it.

—What interests me is why someone whiter than Mary Tyler Moore's pantiliner would be – yo! – chillin' on the Tusc *at all*. Can't quite locate that point on the Cadogan Penn lifestyle bell curve. Any thoughts?

They swerved into the driveway. Hey! cried Penn, clearly grateful for a change of subject, we're home! And, because the *entire* staff has ankled, I got to do this damn code thing myself. No remote! Would you believe that?

Penn leaned out and punched up the number on the silver keypad below the grille on the gatepost, drove through.

—Oh, I'd believe just about any old thing, said Lyn. As long as it's not you.

They parked out front of the house and Penn skipped up

the steps and unlocked the door. Inside, he dropped the keys on a Louis Quinze hall table with showy nonchalance. He winked at Lyn, displaying his handsome white teeth.

—Know what I like about you? he said, making a fist in front of his face. You're *feisty*. I *like* that.

—Oh, god, Lyn said, rolling up her eyes.

—So! Pancakes! Wanna see if we can hunt down a kitchen? Place like this, there must be millions of 'em. He opened a door at random.

—I'm not here to toss pancakes, Penn.

—Sure you are. Oh, I get it, you mean not *here*, in this room. That's true. It's a drive-thru hall closet. With factory-fit *pastels*. Mm. I should have let him take his clothes. I should have insisted. Jesus, there's all his underwear upstairs. You know my trouble? No eye for detail. I get excited. Are you excited? Is this a kitchen yet?

Penn continued gabbling until they found the kitchen, his voice echoing through the vast spaces. Lyn remembered Usher's description of it as an empty box of bricks and wood. The more Penn's voice filled it, the emptier it sounded.

The kitchen, when they found it, was not on the same Brobdingnagian scale as the rest of the house, and the beat-up old table covered with newspapers, the comfortable kitchen chairs, untidy bookshelves and portable TV all suggested it had been a lived-in space. Paradoxically, Lyn felt even more ill at ease here than in the big rooms, as if she was intruding, breaking and entering, there by false pretenses. It was like Usher had just slipped out, could come back at any minute. Lyn hoped that he would come back, returned to his senses, bounce Penn's buns all the way to Tuscadero.

—Old Ed did his own cooking, Penn said, so I didn't

have to sack the cook. Can you believe that? Cooked for himself. That's like being poor.

Lyn sat on a high cane stool at the island workspace, slab marble top lit by low copper-shaded lamps, and toyed with a corkscrew in the shape of a fish. I don't agree, she said. This is the only part of the house that has some identity to it, doesn't feel impersonal. It's where he did something he enjoyed, and it shows. And where *is* the poor man? Where did he go?

Penn was opening closets, pulling stuff out. Actually, he said, I think he went to deliver a letter. Don't feel too sorry for the guy. I didn't leave him exactly destitute. He's got enough scratch in his mystic number bank to build himself a couple more places like this. Took the butler guy with him, press his pants, iron his newspapers. You know what he said to me, the butler, whatever he was? He said, *And on a personal note, if I may, sir, I urge you to fuck off.* Charming.

—Good for him, said Lyn. Right on the button. You stole his home, and you kicked him into the street. How do you expect him to feel toward you? Warm and fuzzy?

Penn froze, a mystery kitchen utensil in each hand. Okay, he said with a tired sigh. Let's get this straight. One more time for the world. Ed Usher was completely happy to hand this place over to me. I do not and *can*not force people to do what they don't want to do. My clients always get the best deal of their lives from me, and they'll be the first to say so. This thing in the box is the real deal. It can remove facial tattoos, correct inappropriate behavior, and make the blind to walk.

Penn warmed to his theme, gesturing expansively with the utensils. And, quite apart from anything else, he said, and

I've only just thought of this, it offers absolute incontrovertible proof that *religion* is just a bunch of sleazy sales teams with no product. Earl Corrigan is a fucking saint compared to those guys. At least you *do* actually get a set of remolds from him, you're not driving around on your bare rims pretending they're tires, telling people how nice and spongy and safe and hardwearing they are. If you're after a real scam, go after the churches, the temples. Any religion will do. You know what a church is? The real empty box. Only thing in a temple is a bunch of towel-heads looking for what's not in it, looking up each other's butts. This box actually *does* what religion has absolutely failed to deliver, and you don't have to grovel in guilty self-abasement to get it. And also you don't have to die, which is kind of like its USP. You just have to be rich! What could be more democratic, more *American* than that?

Penn broke off, surprised at his sudden and impassioned volubility. It wasn't what he'd set out to say at all, but it had been a good tangent. Then he remembered what had got him worked up in the first place.

—I am *not* a thief, he said. So don't ever call me a crook ever again. Got it? Or you'll be writing your story on the sidewalk. In colored chalks.

There was an unpleasantly charged silence. Lyn returned his stare without backing down. If you're so upfront about it all, tough guy, she said quietly, how come you won't tell me what you were doing downtown in the first place? Where does this story really start?

Penn put the utensils on the marble surface and sat down opposite her, ducking his head to see her beneath the lamps. Presumably, he said, you found that Dupree's account backed up my own in every respect?

—Yeah, but . . .

—Well, that's as much as you need to know right there.

—Not quite. Who is the green-haired punk?

Penn rubbed his face with his hands. Maybe to hide his surprise, Lyn thought.

—This is not for your story, right? Strictly off the record?

—Maybe.

—Or maybe I don't tell you.

—I can always find out elsewhere.

—I doubt that, I really do. Hey, your call. If I tell you, you keep it to yourself. If I don't, you won't find out. It won't affect the story, but at least it'll get you off of my back.

—Okay. Tell me.

—Promise not to tell.

—*Jesus*.

—C'mon.

—Okay, already. I promise.

Penn took a breath, examined his fingernails. Lyn wondered if all this method acting was so ingrained he didn't notice it anymore.

—He's my stepbrother, he said softly, by my mother's second marriage. He's gone off the rails, drug problem, and I was asked, *by* the family, to go talk with him. He's like the skeleton in the closet, you know? I'd like to keep it quiet so my mother isn't upset. This is god's own truth I'm telling you. I want my family kept out of this. He has absolutely nothing to do with this story you're following, other than to explain what I was doing down there. God's own truth.

Lyn considered this god's own truth. The expression had been as superficial as ever, but the content had the ring of conviction to it.

—You know where he is now? Tyler said he's gone.

Penn shrugged, gazed around the kitchen as if looking for him there. No idea, he said. We're not real close. Can we get off this subject?

Although this revelation didn't nail down all the loose ends, it came pretty close. And, she realized, it was as much as she was going to get out of him. For the moment. She decided to take him at his word, making the useful distinction between that and believing him. But she didn't make the pancakes, compromising by giving him very simple step-by-step instructions. In pancake-making, too, she suspected he knew more than he was letting on. They cleared a space on the kitchen table for their plates and a cafetière of blue mountain coffee, beans ground by herself as some kind of concession.

—So, tell me the Lyn Crowell story, said Penn through a mouthful of pancake. I got three minutes.

—You're not interested. This is just a patronizing and totally transparent attempt to get me to like you for some reason. This whole evening. The whole lovably inept male-in-the-kitchen ploy. And guess what? It's not working! Can I get more coffee here?

Penn poured her some coffee, looking at her critically. Historically, he'd always gone for blond, but this style was kind of sophisticated, he had to admit. But her eyes were her strongest feature, long and just very slightly cruel. Intriguing. He liked the spark in them when he irritated her.

—So, Lyn Crowell. You're from where, Utah? Where's that?

—Uh-huh. That's like in Belgium, next to Rome? Where the Eiffel Tower is. We got kangaroos in the woods. It's nice.

122

—Got a boyfriend back there skulking in the undergrowth?

—Not like this is any of your beeswax, but no, I don't. Not since he became more of a stalker than a boyfriend. One reason why I'm so glad to be out here with all the normal people.

—And you wrote a story for the newspapers, which made your name a byword for brutal integrity and penetrating insight.

—I did a long piece for the local paper which was picked up by a national agency and widely syndicated.

—Yeah. I don't think I saw that.

—Well, I guess that's because *Lui* didn't run it.

—Topline me on it anyway.

—There was this guy, Gary Wilder, who disappeared into thin air. Several responsible citizens, including some republicans, claim to have seen him fly or float off into the sky, and there's a growing cult of brain-lite idiots waiting for him to come back and tell them what heaven's like. They've made a church out of an old radio station in the desert. Beam up messages to him.

—Doesn't sound particularly newsworthy to me, said Penn, brow creased in thought. This is LA, though. Maybe if it was Woody Harrelson. In a quiet week. Penn laughed suddenly. Kind of ironic that your man Gary's up there in heaven and god's down here lurking in a shoebox. Maybe he got tired of Gary relaying all these radio requests, wanted a bit of peace and quiet. You got to laugh, right?

Lyn didn't look as if she was laughing. She said, You don't seriously believe you've got god in that box, do you?

Penn raised his hands in a mime of innocence. I don't know what's in the box. I haven't looked, right? I just go by

123

my clients' feedback. God is used as a model with reassuring regularity. I don't *believe* anything. But then I don't have to. Whatever it is, it seems to tick over nicely without my sacrificing goats and mumbling dead languages in a dress. It works, what can I tell you? Take a me pill on this.

—But you can understand how it's going to be received by the reading public out there. Good generic loony-tunes stuff. Flaky old LA scamsters.

—Why, *thank* you for your old-timey backwoods courtesy.

—You're welcome.

Penn dropped his fork noisily onto his empty plate. You know what I see here? I see a nice, smart kid, played here by Sandra Bullock before she did *Demolition Man*. I see a decent rural community, like *Little House on the Prairie* without the unpleasant undertow. Father (an award-winning cameo from Gerard Depardieu) hoes the beets at night with his rooty old hands to put her through college. She skips to the big city with only a college diploma and a brown-bag beet lunch, and she's suddenly hurled into a world of glamor, excitement, and fourteen types of coffee, none of which she can pronounce. Aroogah! Zeitgeist overload! She can't handle it. So she adopts this hardboiled, cynical hick-that-ate-Tokyo persona to deal with it. So she can't be reached. But mild-mannered Cadogan Penn with his secret pet-telepath vision, he sees through this gnarly outer layer to the vulnerable, sweet kid inside. A kid who's in real danger of withering away to dust in there . . . I'm sorry, but it hurts me to see this. It hurts.

Lyn, who'd been smirking since the words *decent rural community*, poked her fork at him. And hey, you know what? she said. I'll just *bet* you reckon you're the one to help me

reach within and nurture that inner child, Penn. And I'll bet
it involves, oooh, succumbing physically to your outstand-
ingly studly presence somewhere along the line. Am I so
very far off the track with this? You're imagining some
primal scene of animal lust that will turn me into a dewy-
eyed and grateful girlie acolyte? Sit at your feet and catch
your cigar ash in my teeth?

Penn considered for a while. See? he said. It doesn't sound
so bad coming from you. So – whaddya say?

—I urge you to fuck off, Penn.

—Okay. Want to watch some TV?

—Are you kidding?

—Check out a client of mine. Although he doesn't know
it. Come on, it's for your story. Bring your girl reporter's
notebook and the glasses.

Penn took a bottle of Burgundy from the rack and they
went into the TV room. The set was in an antique cabinet
with a semicircle of Liberty print armchairs around it. Penn
flopped into a chair and aimed the remote. Lyn took the
bottle from him and poured a couple of glasses, gave one to
Penn. Perfect timing, he said, setting fire to a Davidoff cigar
from the humidor. Here's someone else who's looked in the
box and hung around. You should talk to him. I didn't steal
his house. Mind you, I'm not sure I'd want to.

Lyn saw Shuggy Kristiensen's bald head loom up on the
screen. Shut up, will you? she said. This is weird . . .

Shuggy Kristiensen was a changed man. Last seen shedding
his rug in a state of wordless wonder, he'd been called to the
studio by some very worried suits who thought he'd been
somehow drugged on-set, and had sent out immediate PR
on that basis to excuse his inexplicable behavior. It didn't do

125

the ratings any harm; in fact, figures were significantly up for the next show. The suits didn't understand what had happened, but they'd been reassured by Shuggy's performance in the office. Lucid, calm, quietly humorous, he put them immediately at ease. Change of life, he said. The show would go on, and he was very much at the helm.

When he turned up for work, the change of direction was immediately apparent. He arrived early, spoke to the freaks on the sidewalk, asking them questions and listening attentively to the answers. When he opened the show, it wasn't with the usual heavy innuendos and face-pulling, but an unscripted talk straight to camera.

—Hello, and a mystic Shugster handshake to all you stripsters and hipsters out there in la-la land. Yeah, I know what you folks have been hearing. The Shug-man's giving out flowers at the airport. Well, there are going to be some changes on the show, especially up top – he patted his bald head – and I'm sure you're going to love our new direction. I guess what I'm saying is that I've realized that I've been kind of on the wrong tack for a few years, what we've been doing down here.

—The problems here on the wrong end of the Strip, and the people that got them, they're not entertainment. They're real, and they're not getting any help. So before the good people in the suit room pull the plug, we're gonna be meeting people that got something to say, right off the Strip, and we're gonna get some pretty strong stories here.

—In a few seconds we'll be talking to a couple kids sleeping in a refrigerator box tonight, but right now I'm making a special request to the guy out there with the *other* box, yeah, that's right, the guy who you all saw right here on our last show. The box guy. I'm asking him to come

126

forward, or anyone that knows him. There's a reward, five thousand big Shuggydollars, that's right, you heard me and I never lie, that's five thousand tax-free bucks, because he may not know what he's got, and it's real important. So, before we welcome our first guests tonight, we've got a kind of auction set up here to get things moving. The famous Shug Rug, the ol' pompadour d'amour. I'm never gonna wear it again, and the highest pledge we get during the show, that's gonna win this unique bit of hair history, and the proceeds will go direct to our first guests tonight . . .

Penn hit the mute button. Jesus, he said. The poor slob just stepped on his own hose.

—Maybe not, said Lyn. Looked pretty vital to me. That straight to the camera stuff was straight from the heart too.

—Yeah, but Earl Corrigan, what does he care about the homeless? What do the morons out there with the itchy butts and tubs of chicken parts care about kids living in a box? It's depressing. This is a nuts-n'-sluts show, not a fucking Hillary Clinton tofu hug. I always hated the guy, I have to say, and I wish him well, but he shouldn't have fucked with the formula.

—You got a donor card?

—Huh? Why?

—They're going to be *real* disappointed in the cardiac ward. Anyway, I'd rather listen to him, or anyone actually, than you. So stop being so male with the remote, okay?

—It's my remote. And being so male is what I do.

—Oh, please. Just stop. Go drive your cars into the pool or something. I want to watch this.

Penn held out the remote for her, snatched it away when she reached for it.

—Fun-ee, she said. You know your problem? You're not non-seizing enough.

Penn stood up and dropped the remote in her lap. I'm going to try on some new rooms for size, he said. I'm bored with this one. He left her watching the new, caring Shuggy show. Well, he thought, who'd of thunk it. He strolled out into the hall, letting his fingers trail over the brocade upholstery, the French-polished walnut, the ormolu, the gilt pictureframes, the thick, waxy brushstrokes of the paintings. And here were suits of armor, dark and cool, and tapestries like medieval cinema screens, before they could move the people about.

All mine, he thought, sighing with deep satisfaction at a staircase you could sail an America's Cup yacht up. That brass stair-rod there, that's mine. That gold-plated plug socket. That's mine. He walked up the steps and along a galleried corridor, windows along one side looking out over the garden. Chinese porcelain vases in the windows with dying flowers in them. They're mine. Discarded copy of an Arthur Hailey novel dropped by one of the guests in flight. That's mine. He looked into each room in turn, lost count of the beds, the baths . . . *my* property. He buried his face in velvet drapes. Silver-framed photographs of smiling people on a piano. He played a couple of bogus jazz chords. *Mine.* Wall-safe full of money. Mine, too. This black oak gun-cabinet, these shiny pistols. I own them. He spun gold faucets, watched the steaming water splash, powered up chandeliers, dimmed them down, adjusted beds electronically, switched on all the TVs he could find, the music centers, flushed toilets, opened closets, fell off the Nordic Track and set the sauna on stun.

All mine! he shouted, flopping back finally on a four-poster bed in what he guessed to be the master suite. The stained-glass window glinted warmly, the leather-bound books in the walnut shelves glowed, the lacquer boxes on the dressing table gleamed. This was home. This was his milieu. The phone rang and he picked it up, expecting maybe Lyn on an internal line.

—Hel-lo, he sang. Citizen Penn in the master bed—

—I been talking with Ed Usher, interrupted a disturbingly familiar voice, heavy and unsmiling. He's told me some shit, and I think we better take a meeting.

Penn sat up, suddenly wide awake. I'm sorry? You are?

—Don't fanny around, kid. This is Fabio Cicoira. Ed tells me we met already, but forgive me, I meet a lot of cheap hustlers.

So Usher had kept his word. The next stupid-faced cash cow rolling on up for a good milking. Yeah, said Penn, we met at Le Park, Mr Cicoira, only I'm afraid I didn't get your name.

—You got it now, asshole.

—And you're forgiven. When can we meet?

Cicoira gave him directions to an address up on Crescent Drive and told him nine-thirty. Exact. Penn replaced the phone and punched the air. Yessss!

—Enjoy your little tour? Lyn was sprawled on the couch, empty bottle of wine on the floor. The lavender skirt, Penn noticed, had ridden up to show more leg than he'd realized she had. And, like Chinese vases, much more desirable as a pair.

—Mm. Tell you what. Pick a room. Purely for journalistic efficiency. Call it your operations base.

—How romantic, she slurred.

—You want romance?

—Hell no. I want operations base. For operations.

—Still taking the swine-flu remedy?

—Ate the last TriPansodol this morning. I think. Or just now.

Penn picked up the wine bottle from the floor and set it on the table.

—Let's hope you sober up for the big day tomorrow.

—You're giving New York back to the Indians?

—Not exactly. I just fielded a call from a guy named Fabio Cicoira . . .

—Sounds my type already.

—And tomorrow I'm going to teach him some manners, and he's going to give me all his money. Every last plugged nickel. And you're going to be there to see it happen. So let's get some sleep, huh? I got first dibs on the master suite, but hey, buckle up a suit of armor if you're concerned that you may yield to primal urges.

Lyn had just pulled the sheet over her head when she heard the knock at the door. Real predictable, she thought. What? she said.

—I got something for you.

She waited, thinking, sure you do. Bottle of champagne and a boner to balance the glasses on. She grunted, I don't want it.

—I'll leave it outside your door. It's just here. 'Night.

After maybe three and a half minutes her curiosity got the better of her and she unlocked the door. On the floor, a shoebox, tied with glittery gift twine. She knelt down, hearing her knees crack, and looked at it. Was it the same box? Looked like it. Ampar label. Made a mental note to

130

trace the shoe company. She looked up and down the corridor. Eerie moonlit emptiness, silence, fan of light from her room bringing out the colors in the carpet. She put a hand out, touched the box, expecting Penn to whisk it away on a wire or something. No wires.

She picked the box up with both hands, put it down right away with a shiver. *Something* moving in it. That mythical beast stuff. He'd put a mouse in it. Stupid annoying trick, whole thing was just a trick. Her heart pounded. She bent down slowly, listening, hearing only her heart. Bent closer, put her ear on top, holding her hair out of the way. Silence. She sat up, crosslegged, staring at the thing. Is it a bomb? She knew nothing about this Penn guy, when it came down to it. *Nothing*. Biting her lip, she very gently, very carefully, picked it up again.

No, she decided, it wasn't an animal in there. When she held it still it felt light enough to be empty, but when she moved it there was this almost liquid resistance which shifted the balance, then faded. Just like Penn had said. She sat and stared at it for a long time, moving it from time to time, just to feel it. Then she made her decision.

In the morning Penn sat at the kitchen table in terrible-looking Hawaiian silk pjs, drinking coffee and smoking. He looked up briefly as Lyn came in. She was wearing the same stuff, of course, but looked pretty snappy, if a little tired under the makeup.

—So, he drawled, feigning interest in a newspaper. We resisted the temptation last night.

Lyn helped herself to coffee. Temptation? Don't flatter yourself.

—Oh-ho, but forgive me, I don't think I do, said Penn,

with a smile she wanted to wipe off with a cheesegrater. You didn't look because you *believe me*, see? Think about it. He blew smoke down his nose. You and I, we've more in common than you care to think, Miss Crowell.

TEN

Pitch Jitters

—Are you sure this is it? asked Lyn, squinting over her sunglasses at the hedge Penn had parked alongside.

—Sure I'm sure. I know my Hollywood. This place was built for Faye Eden. Party girl in the 'twenties? They found her rotting body in her bed in 'sixty-five. Room was full of birds. Nice to know you got neighbors, huh? What time do you have?

—Show time. Wow, mysterious or what?

A section of hedge had swung open to reveal a brick pavior driveway. They drove through and the gate closed behind them, branches meshing seamlessly.

—Not bad, said Penn grudgingly, eyeing the brilliant white confederate architecture of the house, although a little cramped for my tastes.

They were shown into an airy, high-ceilinged lounge and told to wait. After ten minutes of fidgeting Penn got up and started pacing back and forth. He can't treat me like this, dammit.

Lyn said nothing. On the way here Penn had kept referring to the meeting as a pitch or, worse, a *hit*. He'd said he was going to do a direct *disclosure*, and Lyn was to shut her eyes when he said the password, which she'd forgotten. The disclosure was key, he'd said, and he was working on

133

another concept for this but wanted her to witness the direct disclosure first. She'd tried to block all this stuff out, as his vocabulary made her jaw seize.

She watched him fasten and unfasten his jacket and fidget with the handle on the aluminum photographer's case that held the shoebox. That wasn't enough to occupy her mind, so she gazed out of the window.

There was that ominous, heavy feeling in the air she'd noticed at Arkady, by the pool. Nothing moving outside amongst the hard brilliance of the green and the blue, and only Penn's fidgeting fighting against the white silence that saturated the house. The case handle flopping over and back. Penn sighing, pacing the room, face like fury.

—Nine-thirty exact, he said, like it mattered? No trades, either. But I guess *Made Guy Monthly* is about his limit.

At last, at just before ten, the door opened, and a faceless heavy intoned, Mr Cicoira will see you now, this way. They followed him down a pale-green corridor and into Cicoira's office, a big dull cube of a room with wintry landscapes on the walls and snootily hostile furniture.

Cicoira was on the telephone, staring out through the French windows into the garden and grunting occasionally, using a toothpick. He looked, Lyn thought, too big to be inside. Like he didn't fit. His head was huge, a bull's head, and his profile, the way he sat, reminded her of the Minotaur. She'd seen a painting, when a little girl; the Minotaur seated like that, looking away. What had given the picture its power was the feeling that the beast was about to turn around, and you didn't want to be there when it did. She got exactly the same feeling now. The door closed behind them. Penn went to say something, but the sound dried in his throat, turned into a cough. A minute or so passed. Penn looked darkly at

Lyn. She shrugged, walked across the room and sat in one of the buttonback chairs waiting at a subservient distance from the desk. Penn went to join her. Cicoira hung up, went on staring out into the garden.

—Uh, Mr Cicoira, Penn started. Cicoira turned his great head to face them, and Penn's voice, again, faltered to silence. Cicoira let the silence hang for a few seconds. Then he spoke, in a soft, leathery rumble Lyn had to strain to hear.

—Ed Usher is about the best friend I have, he said. You should understand this. He's telling me this fantastic story, something I find frankly hard to believe. He gives his house away – Cicoira spread his hands toward them with an expression of wide-eyed astonishment – his beautiful house, that he built for his beautiful wife. This, to me, this is incredible. You should know that Paula, rest her soul, was a very good friend of mine also. We go way back, way way back. So I'm naturally concerned at what is occurring here. We're like family. So Ed's telling me this, this *bullshit*, and I'm looking at him like he's crazy, but he don't look crazy. Seems pretty happy about it, tries to . . . *reassure* me. Wants me to meet the guy that hosed him for his house. Sure. I'll meet the guy. I figure, what have I got to lose, right?

Penn gave Lyn's ankle a knowing tap with his toe at this point. Cicoira shifted his basilisk gaze to her.

—And you are?

Lyn went along with the line Penn had fed her in the car, smiling awkwardly. Um, Lyn Crowell? I'm Mr Penn's assistant.

Cicoira swung his whole body slowly around to stare at her, his bulk making the chair creak. Again Penn went to speak, but Cicoira held up his hand. I'm talking to the lady. They both waited for him to say something. He didn't.

When he rotated back around to look through the French windows, Lyn's head dropped in relief, neck muscles aching.

—You have the contract? Cicoira said tonelessly. Penn, grateful for the input, took a white envelope from his jacket pocket and put it on the desk. Cicoira didn't look at it, said, This is the same piece of shit, excuse me, as Ed signed?

—Pretty much, said Penn, finding his voice. There are necessarily—

Cicoira raised his hand again. Not as far this time, really more just a finger, because they were learning fast. He stood up, and Lyn heard the relief in the chair as he eased out of it. He came around the desk and stood between them, his back to her. This meat mountain in the biggest suit she'd ever seen in her life, eclipsing the sun and filling her field of vision. She couldn't hear what he was saying. But Penn could, shrinking back in his chair, gripping the handle of the case in his lap so hard it hurt. He could hear every softly spoken word. And he could feel the toothpick as Cicoira slowly pushed it through his shirt into his chest, holding it near the point so it wouldn't break. Penn was nodding like a fool, gritting his teeth, trying not to yelp. When Cicoira moved away Lyn saw that Penn was sweating, and noticed the red spot spreading on his shirt.

—Let's go, Penn said under his breath. His eyes were wild. Cicoira was standing at the French windows. He opened the door and flicked the toothpick into the garden.

A minute later, as the car swept out onto Crescent Drive, Lyn broke the silence. So. That went well.

Penn pulled his shirt front so it wouldn't dry to his chest. That fucker. That cheap fucking hood.

—What did he say?

136

—Essentially, he suggested I'm going to revert whatever deal I made with Usher.

—He's not interested in the box?

—*No*, he's not interested in the fucking box.

Lyn felt like slapping him, let it go. And you're going to give Usher his house back?

—What, are you crazy? Give my house away? Just because some fucking Italian acts like a hard-on? It's outrageous. Who the fuck does he think he is? Trying to steal my fucking house.

—Take me home, Penn.

—What, drive to Utah? Are you nuts?

—Auburn Cord's apartment, you dummy.

Penn paused, softened the tone in his voice. Hey, tell you what, stay at the house. Your operations base.

—I need a change of clothes and a change of air. You're getting stale on me, Penn. I need a break.

—We can pick your stuff up. Hell, I'll buy you whatever you need. Let's go shopping.

—What do you think I am? Julia Roberts?

Penn tried a couple more times to get her to stay at the house but his ability to swing a deal today had clearly bottomed out. He dropped her at Auburn's apartment and drove away feeling stupid and weak and something else he didn't quite understand. So he sidebarred that particular emotion and hung a lantern on the stupid and weak. His phone beeped. Yeah. What.

—Yo, Cad Penn. Tyler Dupree.

—What is it, Tyler?

—Hey, panties in a wad or what?

The line was breaking up, so Penn pulled over and got

out of the car, staring at the *LA Times* dispenser on the sidewalk outside the Starbucks coffee shop on Melrose.

—This is not a good time for me right now. Tell me something I love.

—Uh, I doubt it . . . the Wolverine, man, Joel's had to hustle his bad self off of the street. *Crazy* people after his ass. Shuggy . . .

The line hissed with static. Tyler? Wait up, I'm in cell hell . . . hey? Have you got me?

—Some stupid *re*-ward . . .

The line broke up completely just as Penn saw the headline. He hunted frantically for change and fed the slot, ripping the paper in his rush to get it out of the box.

Irv Mance mourns son, 39, drowned at Manhattan Beach

The body discovered two days ago on Man-hattan Beach has been identified as that of Dean Mance, son of Irving Mance, the movie producer . . .

So it went. Penn found it hard to focus. It seemed like huge invisible buildings were collapsing soundlessly all around him, black helicopters beating the air with insect wings, swarming for the kill. It was time to crawl into the dark.

ELEVEN

Lard-Baby's Line of Slime

Auburn Cord's apartment felt as if nobody had lived in it since disco. Lyn turned the TV up loud and hit the bathroom until she felt human again. She slung on her kimono and checked her messages. *Beep*. Her stalker ex, a kid called Farrell, calling from Larry's Lunch Pail at Saint George, too high to grasp the principle of the answering machine. *Beeps*. A bunch of short, monosyllabic *ur*-girlie calls for Aub, which were, as far as Lyn could tell, entirely devoid of content. *Beep*. Her editor at the *Witness*, asking her to touch base. *Beep*. Her mother giving her a recipe for old-time spice taffy she'd bought from a *Star* classified, repeating all the instructions and giving Lyn time to write it all down. *Beep*. Something for Aub from Dean Mance's office, cut off at the end of the tape.

She dialed the *Witness* and left a message on her editor's voicemail. Then she copied down the recipe so she could say she had, and because it made her smile. Then she made herself a herb tea and sat on the couch with her Powerbook warming her lap, mashed the keys for a couple of hours. To wrap this story up, it was apparent she needed a sharper beginning. On paper, as well as in her head, the finding of the box raised more questions than it answered. She knew she was going to have to take that hike out to Tuscadero

Street. At about one-fifteen she put on some sweat baggies, did her hair up in a coiled silk square, and pointed the Pinto downtown, streetplan punched flat in the passenger seat.

It was almost two when she found somewhere to park near the poolroom, and she was hot and grouchy again. She asked the guy behind the bar if he'd seen Dupree.

—Homeboy's real popular all of a sudden. Nike were just here for a endorsement deal. Mus' be the nigger's winning personality.

—So, do you know where he is?

—Who's asking?

—You don't remember? I was just here, talking with him.

—We get a bunch of white women down here on their own, you understand. No, I don't know, him nor that buggie Joel neither. Gone change the name of this place to the Don't Know Where Joel and Tyler Is Poolroom, save folk's time. Make a big sign over the door.

—Uh, thanks anyway.

—Hey, if you enjoy our service, be sure to tell your friends.

She was walking in the direction of the porn store when she felt a big hand on her shoulder. Dupree, wearing the hood of his sweat up, Elvis-at-Vegas sunglasses, bent to talk to her. Let's cross the street, get out the light, he whispered, leading her to the sidewalk opposite. They ducked into an alley. Excuse the secret shit, he said under his breath. Street's full of bounty hunters looking for the Wolverine, and every nigger thinks I know where he is. Incidentally, this is the exact historic spot where I housed Penn, saw in the box. Right here, you standing on it. His face was right there.

Lyn looked around, trying to picture Penn amongst the

trash. She asked Dupree where the nearest shoe store was. Dupree jerked a thumb over his shoulder. A block back, I guess, he said. Lectronics an' videos an' shit this block.

—So you chased him from a block away?

—Nope, Dupree said, he was out front of this store right here. Used to do business with them, radios, VCRs, that kind shit. Gimme eighty bucks for Cadogan Penn's car stereo.

—Our friend Penn is not telling us the whole truth about the box. And I'm going to find out why. I need to find that punk with the green hair. Would you mind coming with me? I don't feel comfortable going into a porn store on my own.

—Let me ask for you. Ain't no place for a lady.

—Thanks, but this is work. And you'd be surprised how unladylike I can be.

They walked quickly along the sidewalk, avoiding the piles of trash and busted airconditioners. Lyn glanced at Dupree.

—Have you lost weight? You're looking different. You look great.

—I weigh the same, he grinned, flash of teeth. I just ain't the Pilsbury doughboy nigger no more. Every day, I wake up, I feel so phat I got to look in the mirror, make sure it's me. We're here. Want me to go in first?

They were standing under the ragged stub of freeway ramp that hung over the Porn Baron. The windows were boarded over and painted black, covered with torn scraps of posters and graffiti. Dupree pointed to a planked-up door next to it, said, That was where the punk used to live, right over. Lyn took a breath and followed him inside the store. She didn't intend to do much browsing, went straight to the counter. The clerk was bagging up a purchase for a customer, a copy of *Ebony Twinkle Tits Collector's Edition* and a *Brownies and Lemonade: The Outtakes* video. The clerk didn't look like the guy Lyn had been expecting, someone maybe with a love-tire, milky yellow eyes and a scaly scalp, this just looked like a normal kid. She waited until the customer left before asking him.

—Um, I'm looking for the guy used to rent the room above? Punk with green hair?

The kid shook his head. I wouldn't know. You need to speak to Tiny.

—Tiny?

—Yeah. You're not the cops? Lyn shook her head. The clerk turned his head and yelled for Tiny. Lyn shrank away from another customer, pressing up against her. Dupree moved him away. From out the back room, through a shiny black-red curtain, came a babyish-looking guy with a love-tire, milky yellow eyes and scaly scalp. He smiled at Lyn, hands busy in his pant pockets.

—What can Uncle Tiny do for you, princess? Lyn repeated the question while he eyed her up. His lower lip was wet and colorless. He squinted at Dupree for a second. You the cops?

—We're not the cops. I'm trying to trace my sister. She's a runaway. This punk used to rent above the store? He fit the description of someone she was seen with.

—Runaway, huh? I may be able to help. Why don't we just step into my office back there?

—Um, I guess not.

—Suit yourself, princess, but I ain't up for standing around answering questions without a drink in my hand. Been a

142

hard week. Brother fell off of a building, killed hisself. Kinda cut up over it. You want me to help you, I'm gonna be in my office.

He went back through the curtain. Dupree gave Lyn a wary look. She said, Stay close, huh? The office was barely big enough for the three of them, metal shelves, stacks of shrinkwrapped magazines and video cassettes, table with phone numbers scrawled on it, and a fraying chair. It was stifling hot and smelled stale and hoofy.

—Excuse the mess, said Tiny, moving a pile of *Baby Arm Bun Busters* magazines off the table. I wasn't expecting visitors. Why don't you perch your pretty little butt right here? Hey, not you, big fella, just joking.

He slumped back into the chair, swung a foot up on the table, took a noisy gulp from a can of beer. Okay, princess, he said through a belch, let's see what Uncle Tiny can do for you.

Lyn ignored his suggestion to perch, stayed close to Dupree. The punk with green hair, she said. Can you give me any information so we can trace him?

—Well, he ain't here no more. Threw all his stuff out on the street. Was picked clean in sixty seconds. Citizens round here very proud of their clean sidewalks, take responsibility for it.

—D'you know where he's gone? Lyn was finding it hard to talk to someone who was openly staring at her breasts and rubbing his crotch with a can of beer.

—Nah, and frankly I could care less. Your sister, how old is she?

—Could you tell me his name?

—Snakeboy. His name was Snakeboy. Used to call him

Spiderboy, that was my name for him, on account of his face tattoo. Annoyed the hell out of him. *Name's fackin' Snakeboy, man*. Have you ever done any modeling?

—Didn't you have any, I don't know, tenant's agreement with him, under his real name?

Tiny laughed, eyes disappearing in rolls of fat. Tenant's agreement? What would that be? Anyways, guy came by later and paid what was owed, so I'm not losing sleep over it.

—Do you know who this was, this other guy?

—Hey, I'm enjoying myself. Takes my mind off my dead asshole brother. Are you enjoying yourself, princess? I'd like to see you enjoying yourself. I like to see people enjoy, I run an *enjoy* business here. Now, what did you say? Oh yeah. Nice, clean college boy, could of made a very nice buck in the modeling profession. Kids, they don't want to listen to advice in their best interests. I'm telling you what I told him. You could be earning a hundred bucks an hour, maybe more.

He leaned forward, reached for her leg, whispering, If you work with the dark meat here, maybe a little more.

Dupree moved past Lyn and took Tiny's fat neck in his fist, bunching up his chins in his fingers. He pushed him back against the pressboard wall, said, Answer the lady's question, or maybe I be torchin' this shithole with the shit still sittin' in it.

Tiny wheezed for a while when Dupree let him go, rubbing his neck. Okay, okay, calm down, he croaked. Shit. I'm being nice, aren't I being nice? What's the fucking problem? Busting in here asking me questions. Everybody's so fucking touchy. Lemme think.

He coughed, took a gulp of beer. Got it. Name on the

check. Sloan. Arthur Sloan. I remember these things, I keep files of in-demand types. You got a photo of your sister? I know a few little tykes personal . . . I like the kiddies . . .

Back out on the street, Lyn was rigid with fury. I feel *filthy*, she hissed. Absolutely *filthy*. Shit. And it looks like we're just getting further away from Penn. Arthur Sloan? Who he?

Dupree seemed distracted, standing with his face pointed up at the sun, smiling, miles away, listening to something. His name shouted from down the street snapped him out of it. Uh-oh, he said, seeing some kids waving at him. Gotta blow.

—Come with me.

—No, they'd be after your ass too. Gone.

Dupree disappeared. The kids ran past, crowding her into the street. She walked quickly back to her car, visualizing in sharp detail a wrecking ball smashing right through the boarded-up windows of the Porn Baron store, flattening the scum shaping woodies at the shelves, right into Uncle Tiny's nasty little lard-baby face. Then she apologized for thinking like that and drove out to the ocean to get some fresh air.

It took a minute's phonebook work in the Rose Café in Venice to locate Arthur Sloan. Ordinarily, she'd call first to set up a meeting, but she didn't know what she was going to say. Inventing some kind of story to get her in seemed pointless, but neither did she feel she could tell the truth to a complete stranger. Especially as she had no idea what it was. And Paradise Cove was just a cruise up the coast away, according to her map. It wasn't like she had anywhere else to go.

She took an outside table and ordered pasta and sipped

145

icewater. A young black guy at the next table was telling his girlfriend about some new Nike pants he'd bought, with the press-studs up the side? Gone be so *ventilated*, he said. Cool, his girlfriend said. The pasta came, and Lyn ate about a third of it before she started to bloat out. Back in the lot, a very aged black guy was sleeping it off in a shopping cart, skinny bare legs hanging over the side. A cardboard sign on his chest read HELP SEND THIS NICE JEWISH BOY TO COLLAGE. Lyn pushed a dollar bill into his mitten, thinking, If you have to be homeless, better here than Alaska, I guess. She wound the Pinto back onto Palisades Beach and onto the PCH, drove through Malibu, looking at the backs of the houses that fronted the beach.

Paradise Cove was signed, with a big warning that parking was fifteen dollars, down through some woods to the ocean. Lyn swung off the PCH and drove down through the lush foliage, seeing the surf glittering between the trees. Just as she got to the barrier the security guy waved her urgently over to the side and a police car, siren blipping, overtook and skidded to a halt in the parking lot. A woman wearing a navy sweatsuit bent to talk to the cop and he sped off again up the road where she was pointing, toward a group of ranch bungalows half hidden by palms and bougainvillea. *God!* the woman screamed, bent double with fury, fists clenched to her sides. I *hate* it up there! The security guy was at Lyn's window. As they talked they looked at the distraught woman, hunkered down and yelling.

—Welcome to Paradise Cove, he said.

—Right. I'm looking for Columbia Cottages?

—You've overshot. Hang a right on the PCH, right again. Sign for Tommy's Tiki Kabana. I'd say you can't miss it but maybe you just did. Excuse me.

146

Another squad car came down the hill in a cloud of dust, and he went over to talk. The woman in the navy sweatsuit writhed in a fetal ball on the ground. Lyn let the second police car past and turned back up the hill, thinking about what the woman had shouted. *God I hate it up there!* This wasn't the first time there'd been trouble in Paradise, obviously. Back on the highway, she saw the sign right away. Tommy's Tiki Kabana, and underneath, in smaller letters, Columbia Cottages.

Lyn stopped where the road seemed to, and checked her looks in the mirror. Auburn Cord I am not, she said. So what. Tommy's Tiki Kabana was a flyblown beach café that had been the epicenter of a thriving little surfing scene back in the sixties, until private development effectively cut off its access to the ocean. The surfers moved up the beach and never came back. Everything was still waiting for them. The surfboard snapped by Bruce Brown during a particularly nasty wipeout, a sketch of Tommy by Ed 'Big Daddy' Roth, a jukebox unchanged for thirty years, and Tommy himself, still mixing drinks, more for himself now than his customers. He had nowhere else to go, and he didn't object to the quiet life, him and his sleepy Hawaiian lady. Lyn asked him if he knew where Columbia Cottages were.

—If you look through the kitchen back here, he said, through the window? That gate there, the track leads right up to them. You'll have to walk unless you got a resident's key. Looking for anybody in particular?

—Guy called Arthur Sloan. I'll take a Coke.

Tommy took a bottle from the cooler. You're in luck, he said, filling a tumbler with ice. Save you the trip. Art's out on the deck there. Go wake him up.

The deck was built onto the side of the cabin, and you

147

could sit and look at where the surf used to be and fall asleep in the shade. Art Sloan would do this most afternoons, a stack of unread student essays on the tin table. Lyn stood and frowned at him, his neat beard and his jazz shirt, head lolling back, snoring softly. Had to be a mistake. *Him*? she mouthed at Tommy in disbelief, pointing. Tommy nodded, made encouraging shoo-ing gestures.

—Um, Mr Sloan? Arthur Sloan?

Sloan started awake, looking disoriented. Huh? What?

—I'm looking for Arthur Sloan?

Sloan stretched, wiping the corner of his mouth. Well, that's me. Or not, unfortunately.

—How do you mean?

—I guessed from your manner that you expected me to look like someone else.

—I'm confused.

—Don't be. That would be my son. Sloan *fils*.

—There's a part *deux*, then?

—You're looking at him. You'll find the sequel, as it were, up at the house. Number five, back up the track there.

—I'm sorry to have disturbed you.

—And I'm sorry you were disappointed. You may not know about *Art*, but you clearly know what you like.

—I didn't intend to be rude.

—But you weren't. *A bientôt, j'espère.*

—Right. *'Bye*, as the French say. The italics are mine, but you can have 'em. Lyn drank some Coke, waved to Tommy, and edged through the gap at the side of the locked gate. She walked along the road through the trees until she crested a rise and saw the cottages, like matchwood dollhouses stuck in the sand.

148

She recognized Arthur right away, the clean-cut college kid wearing faded Bermudas and loose white tee, walking away from the houses toward the sea, and ran to catch up. He stopped and turned when she called his name.

—Hi, she said, suddenly clueless as to how to follow through.

—Hello, said Arthur pleasantly. Looking for me?

—Yeah. I'm Lyn Crowell, and I'm trying to find somebody called Snakeboy? I was told that . . . She stopped and frowned. Arthur was laughing. What's so funny? she said.

—I'm sorry, I wasn't laughing at you. But I have to tell you that Snakeboy is dead.

—And that's funny?

—In a way, yes, it is. Why were you looking for him? You don't look like one of his crowd.

—That was really between him and me.

—Okay. I'm going for a walk along the beach. Wanna come?

Lyn looked at him. He looked okay. Sure, she said, why not? It was deserted here. The brown smog stain on the horizon had disappeared. She hooked off her tennis shoes and felt the sand, warm between her curling toes. The sky was empty of cloud, the sun just beginning to look a little unsteady in the haze as it sank toward the horizon. Shallow waves coiled in over each other's back, licking the sand into lapis lazuli at the ocean's edge. The air smelled good, and Tuscadero Street seemed like a planet away. Arthur said nothing but looked at her out the corner of his eye from time to time, smiling inscrutably.

—It's nice here, she said.

—Yeah. I like it. Kind of a forgotten little corner.

—They walked onto the slick of wet sand. It's been a long

time since I did this, she said, watching the sand swell up and change color around her feet as she walked.

—Uh-huh.

—You knew Snakeboy, then, she said, keeping the tone of her voice easy and conversational.

—Better than anyone, I guess.

—So how did he die?

—Ah. An accident. A lucky accident.

There was something in the tone of his voice, like he was playing with her, or testing her. She stood in front of him, so he had to stop, and squinted up at his face. Something Penn had said, when he'd been going on about what the box could do. Make the blind to walk. Correct inappropriate behavior. Remove facial tattoos.

—I'm being kind of slow here, aren't I? she said.

He laughed again, and as he looked in her eyes she knew he knew she knew. So this was Penn's half-brother. The black sheep, the skeleton in the closet. And someone else who'd seen in the box. Someone Penn had done his best to steer her away from. And the missing first chapter to her story.

—Slow? he said. Supernaturally quick, I'd say. It's hardly an obvious connection to make. But I'd love to know how you made it.

—It's a long story, she said. Wanna hear it?

TWELVE

This, to Me, Is Tennis

—I deserve this shit, said Penn to himself. In as much as anyone deserves it, I do. He was riding a brand-new Harley-Davidson through the living room, a Davidoff between his teeth and one of the Tammi Triplets hanging onto his back and screeching, Go, Cad, go! in his ear. Except for her bra on his head, they were naked.

Some furniture had been broken, the kitchen was flooded, and there had been a small fire in the television room. The other two Tammis were by the pool snorting coke and sucking a bottle of Chivas Regal and fucking each other in the ass with a strap-on. Penn had set up a video camera so he could catch up later.

—Hey! he shouted over his shoulder as Tammi, screaming, grabbed his cock. Let's go for a swim! He accelerated the Harley through the jungle in the conservatory, smashing down trees, out onto the patio and straight into the pool.

In truth, he admitted, this was somewhat at variance with the hermetically cloistered existence he'd envisaged for himself after leaving Cicoira's house. But there were reasons for the change of tack. A few calls to business contacts had reassured him that Dean Mance had drowned in a riptide while surfing, plain and simple; nobody was asking exactly why he'd decided to rewax his board after a twenty-year layoff. Hey, shit happened.

And, of course, there was nothing like a wall safe full of money and a big empty house to bring out the sociability in a guy. What was he to do, paint watercolors?

The Tammi Trips had been at the top of his shopping list ever since he'd seen them at one of Mance's parties, doing live hardcore for some visiting Japanese. Tammi Latex, Tammi Leather, Tammi Lace. Leather had the strap-on and dog leashes and whips. Latex wore an all-over shiny suit with thoughtful zippered access and eight-inch stilettoes. Lace wore stuff you could eat. Penn was pretty certain he'd flossed with her thong, anyway. There'd been a bunch of stuff going on, and what with the pharmaceuticals and everything he was a little confused right now.

He knew he was under water, he knew that much, so he wasn't totally out of it. It was nice and peaceful down there, just him and the dark blue water and the Harley, belching smoke bubbles. He could see Lace kicking up to the surface, her toenail polish like tiny brake lights. After a while the Harley quieted down and the concept of breathing for a living started to have its attractions. He worked his leg out from under the gas tank and floated up calmly to the light.

—Wow, he said. Everything's so *green*. Did the camera get that? He swam to the edge and hung from the side by his chin, grinning stupidly.

—You crazy guy! squealed Lace, rolling over and over on the grass. What a crazy guy! Is this guy crazy or what?

The other Tammis lifted their faces from the mirror and fell on their sister, sticking stuff into her everywhere. Penn watched them writhe and kick, listening to their little yelps with indulgent pleasure.

152

—Hey! he cried unsteadily. Any more like you at home?

Leather unplugged herself and crawled toward him, the glossy black dildo flashing between her strapped-up thighs. She slid into the water over his shoulder, studs and buckles scratching his back.

—Hey! he slurred. Lesh get married!

Leather was biting his ear, curled around his back, pinching his nipples with enameled nails. Latex held his face between her thighs, wrapping his hair in her fingers. He was biting a zipper open. Leather was working the strap-on up his ass. He was being lifted, dragged, rolled . . .

—Mmmph! he said as a nipple ring pushed into his mouth. He felt grass against his cheek, smudged up against a white chalkline. I have a tennis court? he wondered, feeling lips sliding up his cock, hot tongue. This guy is cra-zee! He's fucking crazy or what!

He was on top, underneath, tight inside everywhere. Little moans, blurred eyes. Pretty boy, fuck the pretty boy. The white chalkline. Lick it, baby. Leash tight around a breast, hot spray of water, sharp-tasting. Shard of a mirror reflecting the sky. Powder mixed with sticky red stuff. Pink guck. Lick it, baby, lick it up. Uhnh. He's a crazy guy! Spank. Zipper, black fingernails. Leather crop snapping against buttock, breast. Mirror again, big shoe, somebody kicking him with a big shoe. Hahaha. Big black shoe. What? Ooofff . . . Tammi Trips yelling, different voices. Hey! Sliding off him, out of him. Hey! Where is everybody?

—Hey! he moaned, rolling onto his back. Come back! I'm lonely. Lesh get married! The big shoe again, kicking him. Big black shadow against a dark sky. Hey!

—Get up, asshole.

Penn blinked unseeingly. Get up, asshole. Somewhere, he

153

was aware of the Tammis, whimpering, slinking off. Getting married, he mumbled. Engagement party. Hahahahaha. The voice told him to get up again. Then everything went dead quiet for a while, and the world whipped about his head, and he was sick. This was funny! A rope of white vomit swung from his mouth. He was crawling like a sick dog, giggling. He pissed himself. Surely they'd think this was funny, the puke and everything? He snorked. He couldn't lift a paw up to smack away the puke, see, because he'd fall over? Jesus, this was funny! Crazy stuff coming out his head, and his ass hurt. Was it night-time or what? Crazy guy! They loved him, and he loved them, and they were going to be married and fuck each other in the ass. Where was everybody? Now he remembered the voice. Get up, asshole. Deep leathery rumble. He guffawed. Fabio Cicoira! He'd think it was funny, the sick dog act. Hey, Fabio! His face hit the cool plastic frame of a lounger, and he rested his head on it. Not to go to sleep, just to wipe the puke off, cut the rope swinging from his lip, not to go to sleep. He cried for a while. This was funny. Crazy guy. Not to go to sleep.

Cicoira looked at Penn's wet, naked body, smeared with puke and blood and nameless filth, collapsed and shuddering on the Yorkstone paving. He could remember Paula instructing the workmen laying those stones, hustling them along, making sure the job was done right. She'd say, I shouted on them. She shouted on a lot of people in those days. Did them all good.

And now this asshole. This punk. Cicoira shook his head, went into the conservatory for the hose. He came back outside, playing out the hose behind him, and twisted the high-pressure nozzle. Penn screamed with shock before he was completely conscious, covered his head with his arms, spluttering. Cicoira hosed him off, then cleaned up the patio, swilling all the crud down the drain. He turned off the hose and went inside.

The living room looked as if someone had ridden a motorcycle through it. Cicoira picked up the furniture like it was Barbie toys, setting it right. A sidetable and a wheelback chair had been smashed up, and he stacked the pieces against a wall, muttering. He straightened some pictures, wiping one with his handkerchief to remove what looked like a wine stain. He gathered up some clothing from the floor and went back outside, threw it at Penn, who was on all fours, groaning. Cicoira said, Get dressed, you're disgusting. He went back in the house.

Penn shook his head, rubbed his face. *This*, he decided, was the worst night of his life. Getting slapped in the head by Joel was a puppy jigsaw by comparison. He wanted to be sick again, but held it in, knowing the next thing to come up would have a pulse. Getting dressed was harder than Cicoira's stare. His clothes made no sense at all, and he was wet, and everything kept lurching off to one side, collapsing like a pack of cartoon cards. And Cicoira hadn't brought him his socks. His feet were all cut up from riding the Harley barefoot. He hated wearing shoes on his bare feet. He started crying again.

He stood up, locking his knee joints, leaned against the conservatory door. Everything was milky, covered with filmy streaks. He rubbed his eyes, wondering if he wore eyeglasses. He just wanted someone to tell him if he wore eyeglasses. Yes or no. Nothing else, just that, a perfectly simple request. Did he wear fucking eyeglasses or not? Was there *nobody* there who knew the answer to this question?

He stumbled through the conservatory, swatting foliage away from his face. In the living room, Cicoira stood waiting for him, dark and terrible, a Soviet statue made of crushed cars. Penn stood swaying for a minute, trying to keep everything in one place, summon up some dignity so this Italian would respect him. His mouth felt like a cave full of burning bones.

—Ah, he croaked. Just getting a glass of water. Please, he added meaninglessly, help yourself. *Mi casa, su casa.* Hahahahaha.

—We have a little business, Cicoira said. Maybe you thought I just talked to you for the company before.

It seemed to Penn that Cicoira said this twice; once off in a Siberian snowstorm and once right in the middle of his head. For no particular reason, Penn found himself studying his own hands; horrible things, muddy jellyfish, twitching sacs of veiny mucus. He stuffed them in his pockets, hoping Cicoira hadn't noticed.

—My hands are perfectly okay. You're going to kill me, aren't you? he heard himself say, thinking, what a cheap fucking line.

—Drink the fucking coffee, said Cicoira, passing him a mug. I want you straight.

—My hands are fine, Penn laughed. Big black shape looming up at him. He eased a hand from his pocket, it looked okay. He exulted. I told you there was nothing wrong with my hands. He drank the coffee. It was very hot and bitter. He kept on drinking the same coffee. He drained it back, but it stayed full. He drank mug after mug, trying to finish it, as a favor for Cicoira, so he'd like him. Then the room tilted, and he felt carpet against his cheek. Cicoira slapped his face, threw icewater, jerked him to his feet, walked him around like he was a puppet. Little Pinocchio, walking and drinking coffee like a real boy. It was really funny. He was giggling. It went on for a long time until it wasn't funny anymore and he just wanted to sleep.

He lifted his head, and there he was, in a bathroom, retching up tasteless brown fluid into the washbasin. He was alone.

—Jesus, he said, shuddering at his reflection in unforgivingly sharp focus. He turned the faucet on and splashed cold water on his head until he felt well enough to know how sick he felt. His jacket was on inside out, and his shirt was done up all wrong, so he got dressed again and cleaned himself up. What time was it? His watch was gone. The events of the day were trying to line up in some kind of order in his head, like panicking soldiers caught dozing by their drill sergeant. Most of the stuff he remembered didn't seem like him at all. False memory syndrome; he'd read about it. And then the massive dark shape of Fabio Cicoira, and his torn-leather voice. Shit. Holy fucking shit! Cicoira was in the house and he was going to kill him. This was unacceptably terrible. Penn shook his head, trying to clear it. *Oh* boy. Oh *shit*. He needed a gun. Silver pistol. Just to say to Cicoira, don't fuck with me.

He crept along the dim gallery corridor, legs like stupid rubber things, down the backstairs to the gunroom. Found the pistol, put it in his pants pocket. Too obvious. He moved it to his jacket pocket. Better. This was horrible! There was a Mafia guy going to kill him, and he couldn't do anything about it except put a pistol in his pocket. A pistol! He barely knew which end to point. He couldn't call the cops. What would he tell them? If Penn wouldn't believe his own story, why should the cops?

Penn skulked through the house, muttering to himself, peering around corners, his hand sweaty around the sharp-feeling grip of the pistol in his pocket. Where was Cicoira? Had he dreamed it? Silent and dark. He wondered how a place so full of stuff could feel so empty. There was a lot of residual chemical panic still swilling around in his head, stuff that made it all click into a black-and-white movie. A game. Making him sweat. He entered the main hall, lit by moonlight falling through the upper windows. Oh Christ, oh Jesus. Along one wall, a row of Fabio Cicoiras, standing silent, still and dark as iron. Penn couldn't move, felt sweat pouring down his sides. The Cicoiras hadn't seen him, they hadn't moved. Penn raised the pistol at the first Fabio, standing next to the door. *Bang*, he whispered. It was a suit of armor. An empty steel shell. Penn laughed in relief, aimed at the next, and the next. *Bang*.

The threat removed, he slid into the living room, crawled between the chairs and tables like a tiger, a panther. *I am the king of the fucking jungle*, he said, cunningly low so nobody could hear. He could hear voices now, and see light spilling from a half-open door. He knew that voice. It wasn't Cicoira, it was Shuggy Kristiensen. What the fuck was Shuggy doing here?

He slid along the wall, peered through the gap. The television was on, and he could see Cicoira's huge dark head above the back of the Liberty armchair. He was watching *The Shuggy Show*. So that was it. Penn did some slow breathing, got to his feet and watched the show through the crack in the door. Some guy was showing Shuggy a measured diagram of a shoebox, explaining the mathematical correlations to the Ark of the Covenant. This was intercut with video clips of people on the street holding up shoeboxes and shouting. Penn leaned on the door and it swung inward.

—Get in here, asshole, said Cicoira. The massive head turned and an eye like a bull's eye fixed him, right through the slit in the door. Penn didn't need telling twice. He walked into the room, trying to look as if he owned it.

—Oh, he said, here you . . .

—Shut the fuck up.

Penn was tired of every cheap hood in the greater Los Angeles area telling him to shut the fuck up in the privacy of his own house. But he shut the fuck up. Play to strengths, right? Cicoira turned back to watch the TV. Penn, ideas dying like flies in the bug-zapper of his brain, struggled to deal with two concepts that got uglier as they got clearer. One was that Cicoira was watching *The Shuggy Show* and they were talking about the box. The other was the shoebox itself, sitting right on top of the television, with its sparkly bow of gift twine.

Penn's face distorted in agonized disbelief. How could he have been so stupid? *Had* he been so stupid? How could this situation possibly get any worse? Cicoira thumbed the remote, and the screen went gray.

—Siddown, he said. Penn sat tentatively in a chair at right angles to Cicoira's, as far away as possible. He put his hands on his knees, didn't want to let him know he'd got a gun. Cicoira said, Look at me.

Penn looked at him. It was a terrible thing to have to do, meet that stare. Cicoira said, This has got to stop, and it's going to stop right here, right now. Everything, this whole thing comes to an end right here.

He paused, letting his words take effect, watching Penn to

make sure he understood, he had his attention. When he was satisfied, he spoke again, pointing at the box on the TV.

—That the box? What you showed Ed Usher?

Penn nodded, once. His head hurt. Cicoira stood up, reached toward the box, and Penn saw his intention with terrible freezing clarity.

—You can look in it, Penn stuttered. For nothing! No charge . . .

Cicoira picked the box up with one hand, contemptuously, like it was a pack of cigarettes. Oh god, thought Penn, please don't. Cicoira started shaking the box, smacking it into his palm.

—*Don't* do that, Penn yelped. Please . . .

—You telling *me* what I can't do? Cicoira's face grew darker, and his jaw stuck out, showing his teeth. His voice rose to a bellow. Telling me what I can do with your empty fucking piece a shit? Penn watched in horror as Cicoira's hand tightened around the box, squeezing the sides in, buckling the lid. You're next, asshole! he barked.

Penn looked at the gun in his hand. Had it been fired? He'd heard this *snap*, like a toy gun. Cicoira was absolutely still, taking little puffing breaths through clenched teeth. Penn said *Bang!* and fired again, pointing vaguely in Cicoira's direction, just to see if it was working. Cicoira looked puzzled, muttered something in a conversational tone. His left knee buckled, he swayed, sat back into the chair, the shoebox still in his fist, like he was looking for somewhere to put it. Penn dropped the pistol, stink of cordite sharp in his nostrils, taste of it in his teeth.

—Oh my god, he said, with the sudden sickening realization of what he'd done. His head was clear. Everything was clear. He'd killed someone for squeezing a shoebox. He

160

knew what he had to do. He sprang to Cicoira's side, levered the big claw of a hand off the box.

He was tenderly crimping the box straight when he became aware of Lyn Crowell in the doorway, her eyes almost comically big in a face drained of color. She put her hands to her face, and a little wordless sound escaped from her throat.

Penn looked at Cicoira, whispering and staring around the room like he didn't know where he was. His shirt front hung in sodden red folds. Penn, in a kind of madness, heard himself say, It's okay, I know what I'm doing. It sounded like someone else. Pinocchio. It was dreamtime. That stupid snapping noise in his head. The strings were cut.

—Oh shit, he said. Oh fuck, oh shit.

THIRTEEN

The Macaulay Culkin Memorial Highway to Who Knows Where

—The phone, Lyn said quickly. We have to get paramedics. And the cops. She glanced around the room. Where's the phone, dammit?

Penn put the shoebox on Cicoira's lap. This had to work, and it had to work now, before Lyn could call the cops, or everything really was over, and that was the fat lady he could hear singing, just for him.

—Fabio, he said, his voice urgent, listen to me, look in the box, *please*, look in the box . . .

—Jesus Christ, Penn! yelled Lyn. The man's dying! Where's the . . .

—Look! implored Penn, tearing off the gift twine. Fabio, *Fabio* . . .

The great head dipped, the eyes dull as stones. Penn held the box up and lifted a corner of the lid under Cicoira's face. Lyn had found the phone and was punching buttons, cursing. Penn squeezed his eyes shut and opened the box all the way.

He could hear Cicoira's breathing change in an instant. He put the lid back on the box. Lyn was on the phone.

—Lyn! he shouted. Look! Look!

Lyn turned, dropped the phone on the table, little voice in it buzzing like broken insect wings. Fabio Cicoira was grinning, crying, hand resting gently on Penn's head, like he was caressing a grandchild. This moment of ludicrous serenity and forgiveness, before his expression changed to surprise.

—Oh, he gasped. Oh, oh! He clawed open his sopping shirt, sunk his chin to his chest, watching. Here they come!

Lyn came closer. As she watched, two bright rivets appeared in the wet red flesh around his nipple, and the bullets backed right up through the ruptured tissue and lodged in the sticky matted hair on his chest. The lesions puckered and closed, like a flower going to sleep. Cicoira chuckled, picked out the bullets.

—Nice grouping, kid, he said. Here, have a souvenir. He offered a bullet to Penn, who took it just before he passed out and cracked his head on the corner of the table.

When he swam out of the murk he found himself slumped in the Liberty armchair, Lyn perched on the arm, mopping his brow with a washcloth dipped in icewater. There was a big dressing on the side of his head. Penn, she said unsteadily, we have to talk.

—Fresh air, croaked Penn. She helped him to his feet, and walked him outside, passing Cicoira on the way. He was sitting on the floor, surrounded by bits of broken furniture, whistling. He looked up and smiled as they passed, and Penn flinched. The smile was almost as terrifying as the stare.

Out by the pool, Penn, haggard and sick-looking, stared down at the red and black and chrome Harley on the bottom, gleaming in the underwater lights. It was late, and he was exhausted and wanted to go to bed. Lyn didn't look too indulgent. She looked as though she knew something horrible and shaming about him.

—You just shot someone in there, she said. How do you feel about that?

—Unreal. Sick. I mean, you know, thank god. You saw what happened. He was going to kill me. He was going to crush that ... whatever it is. Then it wouldn't have, it couldn't have made him well. But I wouldn't have fired if he hadn't been about to crush the only thing that could help him if he was shot. I'm confused. The drugs were making everything like a movie. I feel confused. I didn't know what I was doing when I shot him, I thought it was a fake pistol, blanks or something. I'd already shot him six times, he turned into suits of armor. I thought he was just another empty suit. I wasn't thinking at all. I remember saying *Bang!* like it was a game, and thinking he'd see the funny side of it. But everything was very clear, immediately after, when I realized what I'd done, and I knew what I had to do. That was very clear to me.

—You were doing drugs?

—You've heard of quality time? This was quantity time. I'd gone crazy, all the money, the house, and nobody to keep me company. Just went ballistic. You've heard of the Tammi Triplets?

Lyn replied with a look that said *no* more clearly than words.

—We were going to get married, said Penn. They loved me.

—Oh, stop it. This is really maudlin. I don't want to know.

They were silent for a minute. The sound of Cicoira whistling from inside the house.

—I talked with Arthur today, Lyn said. Your brother, remember? The ex-punk rocker?

164

—Yeah? Well, I guess I underestimated you.

—He was more than a little surprised by what you've been up to. And concerned.

—I do okay.

—Take a look in the mirror, tell me that. You look like hell, Penn. There's someone in the house been shot twice in the heart looks healthier than you. Anyway, Arthur said it was he who found the box, so you must have gone back for it. You lied to me about finding it.

—Didn't tell you the whole truth, maybe.

—You lied.

—Okay. Whatever. Can we talk this through in the morning?

—No. How did you get the box? Haggle with the owner? What's the street value of something that can bring a guy back from the dead?

Penn groaned, curled up on the lounger.

—Face it, Penn, she snapped. There's something called the truth. God's own truth, as you put it. Just tell me what it is, while you still can. If you ever could.

—Okay, okay. The owner wasn't there, so I took it. Just to borrow. I was always going to give it back.

—You were?

—No.

—You got into this guy's apartment and stole it.

—I guess so. But whose rightful property can it be? How can you *own* something like that? People tell me I'm just incidental in all this, like it's nothing to do with me. That what I actually own is a cardboard box, not what's inside. So what kind of grand larceny charge can you hang on me for stealing a shoebox? It's a little less black and white than you think.

Lyn's face stiffened, and her voice got hard and angry.

—Penn, ever since I've known you you've given me glib. Everything you say is goddam glib. You're good at it, and I'm sick of it. You took something that wasn't yours, and profited by it. That's like saying the stuff in the safe is rightfully yours because only the key is stolen. You stole something from somebody's apartment! You're a thief! There *is* no gray area here! I remember you getting a real bug in your ass, yelling at me that you weren't a thief, that all this stuff was rightfully and legally yours. When Cicoira told you to give Ed Usher his house back, you getting all self-righteous about *your* house, like he was stealing it from you. You pompous piece of shit! And it turns out you're no better than the guy who took your radio. Worse. He knew what he was. You're a hypocrite. You may be fooling yourself, but you don't fool me. And if you *are* fooling yourself, you're pretty damn easily fooled.

Penn hauled himself into a sitting position and looked at her. Everything she said was right and true. And shaming.

—Uuuurrghh, he said, thinking. She was hugging her knees, staring at him. Shifting loops of light from the pool moved over her face. She had really nice eyes. Okay, he said quietly, so what would you have me do?

—I should think it's obvious.

—Give everything back? Dean Mance is dead, and, no, I had nothing to do with it. I think I spent a lot of what he gave me already. I took nothing from Dupree except my own radio, and nothing from Tischia or Arthur or Fabio in there, mending the furniture with his mystical regenerative wood-glueing powers. And Ed Usher seemed very happy with the deal. He may not want the place back. Shuggy Kristiensen and Joel, *nothing* to do with me.

—So? Come *on*, Penn.

—You're saying give the box back, right?

—Why are we interested in what I'm saying? What are *you* saying?

Penn stood up, carefully, his hand to the dressing on his head. Lyn could see he was wrestling with some inner drama, his face grinding through the agonies of ethical conflict.

—My head is killing me, he said eventually. You know what? The last few days I've been mugged, punched, pistol-whipped, kicked, stabbed with a toothpick, and screwed in the ass by crack whores. Also I shot someone twice in the chest, and it may surprise you to know that *all* this is new and strange and terrifying to me and I want it to stop.

—So, what are you saying?

—I'm saying, this thing is killing me.

—And?

—And I'm going to give the box back.

—Why?

—Lots of reasons. Because I'm scared I'm not going to live much longer at this rate. Because I'm tired. Because if I don't give it back you're going to tell the cops I'm a thief and *they'll* fuck me in the ass.

—I thought I'd just tell Dupree and the Wolverine at first, Lyn said. Remember his mission? Return shit to their rightful owners? Locked doors mean nothing to that guy. You told me.

—I'm excited by the strength of your position. Deal-wise, I came in on one leg on this.

—And if that hadn't worked, I could always set Shuggy and the howling mob onto you.

—Yee. Not great.

—But that's no reason to give it back. Not *the* reason. It's just more Cadogan Penn self-interest.

—You want me to give it back because it doesn't belong to me.

—And what do you feel about that?

—Obviously you're right. Ordinarily that wouldn't be a motivation for me. Right, wrong . . . it's like an ethics class. I can argue one side or the other. But as you said, no glibbing my way out of this one. Ah, Jesus. Give it back before I shoot someone with bullets that don't have a reverse gear. Can I go to sleep yet?

—No. First you're going to lock that shoebox in the case and give me the key, and then we're going back to Aub's place. Unfortunately, I have to keep you in my sight, so you get the couch. There's just one thing I want you to do . . .

Lyn stood and stared up at him. For Penn, who'd had nothing but people giving him weirdly unsettling stares recently, this was nothing new. What was new was the way he felt about it.

—What? he said. What now?

—Just tell me what you're going to do with the box while you're looking me in the eye, without trying to be smart or funny. Don't give me glib, Penn.

He took a deep breath, paused for a second, looked into her eyes, trying to work out what was happening here. I'm going to give the box back, he said. And you have nice eyes.

Lyn drove him back to Auburn Cord's apartment in her Pinto, insisting he leave the keys to the Lexus at Arkady with Cicoira. He fell asleep in the car, head lolling on her shoulder, which might have been touching if he hadn't been a drooler. She pushed him off with her elbow.

—So, he said, lurching nauseatingly into consciousness, how did you find Arthur?

—I thought he was a beautiful guy.

Penn began to say he hadn't meant that, but sleep covered him like a ton of hot sand. Lyn had to drag him into the apartment and haul him onto the couch. She pulled his shoes off, sneering at the pretentious absence of sock, *so LA*, threw a coverlet over him.

—Welcome, she said, to the Couch of Recuperation. I'm Sister Ordinary, and this is as good as it gets.

She undressed and hid the aluminum case under her bed. Hung the keys on Aub's ceramic ring tree, watched them glinting for a while, wondering how it was that when people knew what was in the box they never looked. That was something else on her stick-it-to-Penn list. How he tricked people into looking in the thing, without giving them an informed choice. Oh well, she could hit him with it tomorrow if he started to get argumentative. What had he said? He'd gone in on one leg? No way. He didn't have a leg to stand on.

First thing she did on waking was hang her head over the side of the bed, check the case was still there. She grimaced at all the wads of Kleenex, sneezed from the dust, crawled out of bed. In the living room, Penn sleeping in a tourniquet of coverlet, pillow bunched up hard in his face, wound dressing trailing away over the floor. She watched him for a while, reminding herself it was too easy to like guys when they were asleep. Even Farrell, the Human Roach Clip, had looked kind of appealing in the dim pre-dawn light. Standing there in just a tee, with Penn asleep, was the closest she'd been to sex for some time. The realization made her feel sour. She showered, dressed, and went out for milk at the Korean store on the corner. The mail had come when she got back, and she went through it in the kitchenette while she waited for the water to boil. Opening an envelope addressed to her in a familiar hand, she yelped in astonishment, slapping a hand across her mouth. From the couch, muffled grunts, Penn stirring.

—Wake up, she said, shaking his shoulder. Mail call. C'mon, wake up. You'll like this.

She dropped an envelope onto his chest. Penn coughed, grimaced, blinked, wiped his face with his hand. He could hear Lyn in the kitchenette, fixing coffee or something. He started remembering what had happened the day before, but it all seemed a long time ago, and pointless going over it all again.

The envelope was full of confetti, spilling out all over. A Polaroid with two smudged lipstick kisses on the white strip along the bottom. The picture showed Tischia Burke White and Auburn Cord dressed as brides, embracing outside a church, with people applauding in the background. They looked fantastically happy. There was a note in there, on lavender-scented paper, and he concentrated to get it in focus. WE'RE MARRIED!!!!!! it said, TOLJA YOU'D BE SURPRISED!!!! They'd signed their names, Tish and Aub, and written the date and SAN FRANCISCO in big curly letters underneath.

Lyn brought in the coffee, chuckled at him frowning at the Polaroid, confetti in his hair.

—Life is full of surprises, huh? she said.

Penn cleared his throat. They're *married*? he said uncomprehendingly.

—You saw that, huh?

170

He sat up, cocooned in coverlet, hair sticking up all over, staring at the Polaroid.

—Yeah. I mean, but who to?

Lyn laughed. To each other, you dummy!

He looked up at Lyn, his face twisted. To each *other*?

—Like I said, life is full of surprises.

Penn stood up, holding the coverlet around his waist, worked his face some more with his hand, sat down again.

—Well, he said unconvincingly, I kind of saw this coming.

—Yeah, *right*.

—No, really, it was becoming more obvious to me. Tish and I, she hadn't wanted to, well *you know*, for some time.

—Oh, right. Any woman who doesn't want to *you know* you, that means she's automatically a lesbian.

—It means she might as well be. As far as I'm concerned.

Lyn put her hands on her hips and eyed him warningly. Are you going to behave yourself today or what?

—I'm behaving! I'm behaving! Yeesh, cut me some slack here. I just woke up, found my girl ran off with another girl. This is a traumatizing moment, a guy finds out his girl married another girl. And it's not like the guy was invited to the wedding or anything. San Francisco, huh? Well, I guess these people gotta go somewhere to get married.

—Mm. You have *standards* here in LA.

—Can I get some coffee here? I mean, if you can stop beating up on me for one second?

In the Pinto again, Lyn driving downtown.

—I still can't believe they're married, said Penn.

—I still can't believe you shaved with Aub's leg razor.

—It was either that or your depilatory cream.

—Thank you for your restraint.

171

—Grooming is important to a guy. And, to be honest, I got kind of an erotic charge out of using her bathroom.

Lyn frowned at him. You're sick, she said.

—Anyway, Penn reasoned, it's not like she'll be needing her razor anymore, if she's the butch one.

—For a guy living in LA you're so behind the times it's unreal. It's not like that anymore, that butch/fem thing. People can be who they want to be.

Penn looked out the window. No, he said, they can't. That's the whole problem. Hey! Tell you what. There's a bunch of great stuff we could do with the box before we give it back. Go to Folsom and open it on Death Row. Zap all the guards, all the cops, all the cons, turn them into saints. Can you picture that? Or we could open it somewhere *really* evil, like a major motion-picture studio. They'd start making wildebeest documentaries right there. Seriously. We could really make a difference on a large scale, not for money. Make the world a better place so the dolphins and the trees can sing Navajo chants to each other. Or, if you'd prefer, zap the clerk at this convenience store up here and get some free gas. Whaddya say? Wanna change the world? Or grab some Hershey bars?

—You know what I want, said Lyn.

—No, I don't. I know what you want me to do, but that's not the same thing. Don't you want to change the world?

—I don't want to force things on people that I'm not prepared to submit to myself. Even if I was prepared to look, I still wouldn't get other people to. Nobody who's looked in it has said, Hey, you got to look in this thing. You always trick people into looking in it, or surprise them with it.

—You're scared to look.

172

—I'm careful. If I was scared I'd be back in Utah herding beets instead of cruising downtown LA with a dangerous maniac and a shoebox that could change the course of history.

—It must be me that's scared, then. I knew it was one of us. Hey, see all this traffic we're in?

—I hope so, as the driver.

—Okay. Work with me on this, I think I got something here. Look at this situation. Everyone dragging their butts along at the same speed, a few yards apart, looking straight ahead, not at each other, maintaining the distance, the same relationship . . .

—What stunning *aperçu* is this leading up to?

Penn turned to look at her, thinking there's something powerfully sexual about a woman driving, the position she's in.

—I have no idea, he said.

They pulled off Tuscadero and parked right out front of the apartment block, to save that tedious skulking around. The wheelless Datsun pickup now had no motor or transmission or seats. Lyn stood looking at it.

—What? said Penn.

—Gary Wilder, the guy who disappeared I wrote about? His pickup disappeared at the same time. Black Datsun. This is a black Datsun.

—Wow. One for Ripley. And there's a church for this guy? Because he drove to LA in a Datsun? I *love* this town. Come on, let's get this thing over.

The door with the suns all over it had a big padlock on a shiny new hasp covering the lock, and a typed legal form

173

pasted to it. Penn said *uh-huh* in a knowing voice and they went back outside around the corner. The windows were boarded up with half-inch ply, a really solid job.

—Dude's *gone*, said a small voice. It was the kid in the Lakers hat who'd offered Penn off-street prices.

—Oh well, said Penn to Lyn, there we go. God's way of telling us something. Can't say I didn't try.

She gave him a look and bent to talk to the kid. Do you know where he went?

—Uh-uhn. The man jus' boarded all his shit up inside. Dude's gone.

—What was his name?

The kid curled his lip. Some *white* guy, he said, like that was enough.

—Is that his pickup out front?

—Wanna *buy* it?

—No, said Penn, we don't wanna *buy* it. Come on, Lyn, let's get out of here before you have to buy back your own Pinto.

They went back to the car. Well, said Penn, where now? Seems to me our good intentions are frustrated.

—Oh, we shouldn't let a little thing like that dishearten us, said Lyn, peering inside the cab of the black pickup. She pulled open the door and poked around in the trash on the floor.

—Usually about now, said Penn pleasantly, I'd be perusing the menu at Le Park, watching beautiful people networking for successfulness.

Lyn emerged from the cab with a bit of yellow paper, smoothed it out on the door. What are you telling me? she said. I'm not beautiful people? Come look at this.

Penn went and stared over Lyn's shoulder, taking a

surreptitious sniff at her hair. It was a flyer for a band, The Afterlife Carnival Choir. There was a picture of four guys in gorilla suits holding guitars, and a line of type which said *Sophisticated Syncopation For Society Soirées.*

—So? said Penn.

—The bottom's been torn off here, see?

—Fantastic. Can we leave, please? I hear animal noises in the undergrowth.

They drove up along Tuscadero Street. So, said Penn, our pet phenomenon in the box back there in the trunk. Do I get to keep him? Kin I, maw? Huh? Kin I? I'd look after him real good an' take him fer walks an' teach him tricks . . . an' I'll call him . . . *Holy* shit! Look at that! They torched the poolroom. There goes the neighborhood. Oh, boy.

The poolroom and bar was a black, gutted, sticky-looking mess. Guys stood around grinding glass into the sidewalk and peering inside. One kid was bending a salvaged chairframe on the sidewalk.

—Wow, said Lyn. What's going *on* down here? And, darling! Do look! There's our other sentimental Tuscadero rendezvous. Saint Onan's Chapel of Masturbating Moody Loners. Care to browse?

—You're kind to offer, but their wildest dreams are my muesli. And may I draw your attention to that bit of unfinished roadway hanging over it there? Unbearably *poignant*, no? Going nowhere, see, like my life with no magic shoebox to give it shape and meaning. It's like a metaphor?

Lyn braked suddenly. Okay, she said, here's how we find your guy, give him his box back.

—You don't give up, do you?

Lyn shook a fist in front of her face, showed her teeth. *Feisty*, she said. Remember?

175

—You can have too much feist.

—Okay. Lean out the window and howl like a wolf. As loud as you can.

—What're you, crazy?

—Just do it.

—Like a wolf?

—Loud as you can. Give it some *feist*.

Lyn hung a U-turn in the street and cruised slowly toward the burned-out poolroom.

—Coach me on this, Lyn . . . What's my motivation?

—Just *do* it!

Penn opened the window, stuck his face out, howled high and lonesome. The guys hanging out in front of the place turned and looked.

—That okay? he said, bringing his head in. Yukon Jack enough for you? What is . . .

—Again! Lyn shouted. Penn did it again. This time he got people telling him to shut his fucking mouth, someone else returning the howl. He closed the window just as a bit of bar stool bounced off it.

—Okay, he said, what was all that about?

—Jus' move your asses quick, said a voice from the back seat. C'mon, le's *move* here.

Penn jerked his head around to stare in astonishment at the figure curled up in a scratty-looking cape on the back seat. Lyn laughed and gunned the throttle. They drove for a few blocks and turned down behind a body shop, parked on the edge of a vacant lot surrounded by shabby windowless buildings of no clear purpose.

—Lyn, couldn't we park somewhere else? said Penn edgily. This is where all the murdered people hang out.

—Tell the Wolverine here what you did. And bring him right up to date.

—Why?

—Or do you want me to?

Joel took his Wolverine mask off so he could look at Penn telling the story. He just sat there and listened, eyes steady and attentive.

—I'm thinkin', he said, when Penn had finished, how you looked at me that time I got in your car, held a piece on you. 'Member that? Looked at me like I was the shittiest piece of shitty trash for stealing your box.

Penn sighed. Yeah, Joel, I know, I know. I *really* know.

—Jus' so long as you *wise* to what you *is*, unnerstan', I don' have no problems with you.

—Joel, I'm wise to what I was. Which is a start.

—Okay, said Lyn. So, Joel, we need the Wolverine's help to find this guy, so we can return his stolen property. His stuff is all boarded up inside his apartment, and we don't know where he's gone. Or his name, just that he's white. *This* may mean something, though . . .

She passed him the torn flyer. Joel looked at it expressionlessly.

—How'm I gone reach you? he said. The Tusc ain't no place to be no more, they torchin' places an' shit. Tyler an' me, can't go home no more, hidin' out. Can't work the street no more. Some blood left a box at the poolroom, Mason there open it, blow up in his face.

—Mason? asked Lyn.

—Nigger what ran the place. Good nigger, never tol' nobody 'bout Tyler an' me.

—Thank you, Shuggy Kristiensen, thought Penn. Here,

he said, writing Arkady's address and his cellphone number on a torn corner of Lyn's roadmap. Once you've got something on this guy, you and Tyler grab a cab up to Beverly Hills. You can hide out there until things blow over. And here's some cab fare. Uh, Joel, you wouldn't have to worry about hiding so much if you didn't, you know, *dress* like that.

—Like what? said Joel, taking the address over Penn's shoulder. Penn twisted around to see Joel wearing a brown windcheater with a torn sleeve and gray pants. Later, white people, Joel said, opening the door and walking away.

—How does he *do* that? said Penn, gesturing inadequately with his hands.

—He's a superhero, shrugged Lyn. It's his job. Any shopping you want to do while we're here? We may not be down here again. I saw a Black Elvis mirror, would look neat in your tarpaper shack.

—Black Elvis? said Penn disbelievingly.

—Sure. Why not? It's like those statues in Italy, black madonna and baby. Elvis is an anagram of *lives*, you see. The second coming. Presleyanity is America's only truly indigenous religion.

—Elvis is also an anagram of *evils*, said Penn.

—And Presley is an anagram of *slerpey*, Lyn deadpanned. Makes you think, doesn't it?

—Nothing makes me think, apparently, said Penn, patting all his pockets for a non-existent cigar case. I do pretty much everything without thinking ahead. Or even sideways. You look like the type who always has the right map in the glovebox, though. Got any cigars in there?

—I don't smoke.

—You're going to have to get used to it. Pretty soon the

178

only place you'll be able to smoke in LA will be in Utah. On your front porch. Or stoop or whatever it's called. Where you sit on a sleeping hog with a rusty banjo, while Uncle Elmer wriggles his six-fingered hands inside your dungarees, dribbling in your hair.

—For god's sake, Penn! Do you make all this up or is it based on experience? No, tell you what, don't tell me. Either way it's just too queaze-inducing. Like a lot of *this town*.

Penn snorted. Oh, *sure*.

—You really like living here, don't you?

—Even if there was somewhere else to live I'd still live here, that's how much I love LA. And my broadmindedness is typical. Tell you what, make a right here. This is Century Boulevard, we're in Watts.

—Lovely.

Lyn made a face at the gray strip malls garlanded with tangled cables on slanting utility poles, slack wires stitching up the dirty wound of the street. Nothing grew here except signs, idiotic images of white glamor, and graffiti; the ever-present crabbed calligraphy of the dispossessed, spreading like veins on a wino's cheek. Out on the sidewalk it was mostly young men, sagging in doorways, scuffing their sneakers on street corners. Occasionally a pair of overweight women pushing a shopping cart, or an old guy poking around in the litter. No families, no hand-holding couples, no animals. No grass, no trees, and a birdless sky the color of Tupperware over a fluorescent tube.

—Yeah, said Penn. This is not a great part of town. Thirty years ago the citizens burned the district down so they could put up slums. Make another right just here.

—Okay, I admit it, I want to get out of here. You've made your point.

—No, I haven't, said Penn. I want to show you something. Another LA miracle, where you'd least expect it. Up here, watch this jerk, Jesus . . . Okay, here we are.

In the hallucinogenic pinpoint clarity of the Los Angeles sunlight, where even a gas pump expresses some kind of beat-up beatitude, there is truly no such thing as the mundane. Entropy here is asleep; the glittering rust, the peeling paint, the stuttering signs on their cable-throttled stalks; these things are beyond time. It seemed to Lyn that here, in the dusty heart of Watts, she was looking at the coalescence of this quality, the hypnotic crystalline stasis of LA.

Ahead of them were three towers, jeweled marine skeletons, spiraling up into the blue. With the airily complex architectural logic of a dream, they flashed with countless colored shards of glass and tile and seashell; organic, impossibly delicate antennae, broadcasting on some alien wavelength.

—What *is* it? gasped Lyn, pulling up to the curb.

—*It*, said Penn, are the Watts Towers. Want the story? Okay. In, I don't know, a hundred years ago maybe, this Italian guy starts building them because he loves LA, and he wants to give the town something beautiful. Something that's just beautiful for no reason; not a church or a business or a publicity stunt. Just something beautiful. It takes him like fifty years and a million seashells and every bit of broken glass and ceramic he can pick up. And naturally, everybody wants to tear it down. The city fathers, the landlords, kids on the street, everybody. The fuck does this crazy Italian think he's doing? What is it *advertising*? They can't buy the product, they don't know what it is. So they hound the poor guy into hiding. Dies broke and forgotten in San Francisco. And, of course, they try to pull the towers down. It's on

TV. The tractor cable keeps snapping, the towers are too well built to be demolished. This is like an LA *first*. And gradually, somehow, people begin to see what he's accomplished here. Now, they're a designated cultural monument, and the *idea* of pulling them down gives Angelenos the dog staggers. When they burned Watts, they left the towers alone.

Lyn looked at them, rising up out of all the junk and the mean ugliness; ecstatic expressions of childlike wonder and joy.

—Beautiful, she said. God, they're beautiful. But tragic; the poor guy!

—When they found him, dead in some flophouse, you know what? He was holding a seashell to his ear, listening to the sea, and he was smiling. And he made all *this*. Not the work of a gray, bitter soul. People didn't understand what he was doing at the time, and they never exactly thanked the poor slob, but they remember his name now. Shit-scared crackers from Buttmonkey, Ohio, bus deep into downtown LA to wave disposable cameras at his work. And my *point*, if you're interested, is that this guy, this wonderful guy, this guy whose name I have momentarily forgotten, came *here* to build them. This is my Los Angeles. Your Plastic City. Let's get something to eat.

Penn had used this tactic, with variations, a few times before. The woman has any brains, drive her into Watts, impress her with your sensitivity, street smarts, *depth*. Trouble was, it was a long time ago he read the guidebook, and he was forgetting more and more. The guy's name, for instance. Still, the Watts Towers had worked their subtle magic for him one more time, he could tell.

They drove out toward the beaches, feeling the atmosphere

of threat get fainter and the sky get clearer with every block, and parked outside a restaurant with a clumsy, gaudily painted Marilyn mannequin on the roof. Her arms were snapped off below the shoulder.

—Here we are, said Penn, Marilyn de Milo. Best cold consommé this side of Watts.

—I only hope it has more taste than the sign, said Lyn. While they waited for their order, she asked Penn for a little personal background.

—From the beginning? said Penn, not so secretly flattered at her interest as he liked to think.

—Why not? said Lyn. We're going for dessert.

—Okay. Spool back with me . . .

—Wait. Wanna put a pin in that? This is not a pitch. In English.

Penn sighed. O-*kay*, he said. I was born in sixty-one in Boston. Not an outstanding year for anything particularly, except the Utah beet harvest was an all-time high, as I remember, everyone was kind of cresting on that. I was born too late to qualify for Baby Boomer bonds, too soon for generation-X slacker angst. You can appreciate how difficult it was to niche, zeitgeist-wise.

—*Penn*, Lyn said heavily, raising a forefinger in warning.

—What. What? Anyway. Father a third-generation corporate lawyer, mother from Big Sur via Girton. Any whiter and I'd be Canadian. My dad had a fast-track into the family firm lined up for me, but he died on a Florida fishing trip when I was ten. They were loading up the boat in the harbor. This guy, a client, was passing a crate of beer over Dad's head and dropped it. Dad never drank, and the guy who fumbled it was holding it deliberately high so as to protect him from its influence. You know, like a joke. He was dead by the time they got him into the ambulance. Massive head trauma. Cause of death. He never drank but beer killed him. Some joke. So my mom and I moved west to Grandma's house, where we used to vacation, and she remarried.

—This would be the guy with the beard, interrupted Lyn, attacking the caesar salad. Columbia Cottages.

—Uh-huh, good old Art. Arthur came along soon after. Anyway, when I quit school the partners of Dad's firm offered me a job, but I was never up for flying a desk. So I bummed around Europe, crashed a car into a tree, came back, started to burn up my father's legacy on a series of misguided but well-intentioned endeavors to get a little brass nameplate on a table at Le Park. Oh yeah. Crashed a car into a truck. I guess I'm just easily distracted. Ten years with nothing to show except promise. This box thing, I thought I'd found the last deal in town. I mean, it should have been the Pope, or a poor black cripple, or Hillary fucking Clinton, but no; the fates choose *me*, spoilt, vacuous . . .

—Don't forget glib.

—Spoilt, vacuous, *glib*, to host the millennium of universal enlightenment. While making a nifty buck on the side. Strange, no?

Lyn sipped her Rioja and looked at him. This wasn't quite the same guy who'd almost bragged her to death on the drive up into the hills.

—Tell me the real reason you agreed to give the box back, she said. I mean the real reason, not what you told me. I know I had the threat to blow the whistle on you, but we're not talking about just any old box of shoes here. That's the kind of thing could drive a guy insane, having something like that. The potential in that, the *power*. Hard to let a thing like that go out of your life, I'd imagine. I'd have thought you'd try anything to hang onto it.

—Uh-huh. I had a taste of that madness. What I told you was true as far as it went. I *am* scared I'm going to kill somebody over it, or it's going to kill me. It's been close. And I did steal it. When I think about it now, I don't know why I did. I have never ever stolen anything before in my entire life. There was just something, I don't know, compelling about it. Seductive. It was like I'd semi-fooled myself into believing I was just taking an empty shoebox, so where's the harm? But I *knew* there was more to it than that; I mean, why take the thing otherwise? It was complicated, and everything happened real quick. In fact, since I took it, it's like too much is happening in not enough time. You know, like time isn't *big* enough to hold all the shit that's happening. I'd wanted to keep the whole thing under control, but it hasn't been possible. So all that stuff I said by the pool, when I looked you in the eyes, was true. Especially the bit about your eyes. And I still have the house . . .

Lyn froze, fork halfway to her mouth, gave him a look.

—Okay, he said, holding up his hands in surrender, I'll *ask* Ed if he wants it back.

They ate in silence for a while, Lyn catching Penn's eye from time to time, staring him out. It surprised her how easy that was, and how much she enjoyed doing it.

—So, she said, edging her empty plate away so she could lean on the table, are you going to tell me or do I have to turn Nancy Drew again?

—What? Why I'm turning the box in like a legit citizen? You're smart enough to realize there's something I'm not telling you, but you're *not* smart enough to figure it out. I

184

like that. Nobody knows except me. Maybe I'll tell you, maybe not. But I am kind of curious who I stole it from, to tell the truth. I don't have a game plan for handing the thing back. I can't blue-sky that at all. Look! Quick . . . getting into that gray Caddy . . . see? Tony Danza! God, I love LA!

His cellphone beeped from his jacket pocket.

—Yeah, Cadogan Penn . . . Hello? Is that you, Joel? What? Listen, go to the address I gave you . . . go to . . . shit.

He stared at the phone accusingly, tilting it to read the LCD panel. I just recharged this sucker.

—This person, who owns the box, said Lyn, I'll tell you something about him. Or her. Remember when you were yelling at me that the real story was with you? Well, the real story is with him. Or her. Naturally you see this whole thing as evolving around you, but I have to tell you I'm not writing up the story that way. The person with the box is the beginning and end of this thing.

Penn dabbed his mouth with a napkin, thinking. Alpha and omega, he said in epic tones, gesturing biblically. With me somewhere in between. With all the other characters in the alphabet. And I'll tell *you* something about this guy. You think you know who it is. You think it's the guy that floated off in a black Datsun. So, you have your own secret agenda here in wanting me to give it back. It's not merely out of altruistic concern for my soul, or your noble crusade for truth, justice, and the American way, right? Your moral high ground is beginning to look suspiciously like a little league pitcher's mound.

Lyn saw the mischief in his eye and smiled calmly. I'm keeping an open mind, she said. So, back to the ranch?

Penn was patting his pockets, teeth bared in a rictus of agony.

185

—You're not going to believe this, Lyn . . .

—Stretch my envelope.

Penn gave a short, embarrassed laugh, put his hand to his face. I've left my wallet at home. I gave all my money to my buddy Joel. My ass is out, as Tyler would say. Jesus, Lyn, I'm sorry . . .

—You want me to pay for the meal you just bought me, she said flatly. Is that what you're trying to say? Penn groaned, peeked at her between his fingers. Give me that line again, she said, raising an eyebrow. You remember, about my eyes.

—You have really nice eyes? You have really nice eyes.

—*Nice?*

—Did I say nice? Gorgeous. Gorgeous eyes.

Lyn fished in her purse, face lost in the shadow of her hair. It's deductible, she said. This is work, remember?

FOURTEEN

What Secret Compulsion Made This Lovely Girl
the Handmaiden to Unnatural Horrors?

Cicoira was sitting on the front steps of Arkady, dressed in an open-neck shirt and golf slacks. Just sitting there, he twisted the scale of the place, made it seem smaller.

—Is it me getting smaller or him getting bigger? Penn whispered to Lyn as she killed the motor. A little of both, she said.

Cicoira stood up, dusting off the seat of his pants. The gang's all here, he said pleasantly, giving them a Cinemascope grin. Lyn took the case from the trunk and followed them through to the garden. The house had been cleaned up and there were fresh flowers everywhere. She caught a glimpse of a white-jacketed figure disappearing up the stairs. Simon? On the patio, sitting around a table crowded with long drinks and fresh fruit, some familiar faces. Joel, in swim trunks and toweling robe. Tyler Dupree in tennis whites and sun visor. Ed Usher, in an Aloha Elvis shirt. And standing a little further back, arms folded, smiling in the shade of the loggia, Arthur Sloan III. The guys did their hellos, each in his own style. Cicoira fetched a seat for Lyn.

—This is, uh, great, said Penn, smiling but puzzled. Shuggy's fixing nibbles, right?

Usher laughed. No, he said, we thought it best if he didn't take this meeting.

—Yeah, said Dupree. Guy has a appetite for publicity we don' share.

—There's still a couple guys missing, said Penn. Tischia Burke White, who I believe you know, Ed; and of course Dean Mance. Tischia went to San Francisco to get married. Dean went surfing.

—Those are just the guys we know about, Cad, said Arthur, pouring Lyn a glass of fruit juice. This thing may have been going on for a long time. I was only the first *we* know of.

—Good point, said Cicoira, popping an apple in his mouth like it was a cherry.

—Excuse me, said Lyn, but I'm kind of excited to hear if Joel managed to track down the owner yet? The box guy?

Joel searched through a pile of clothing by his chair, retrieved a crumpled sheet of paper. Yo' man, he said. Some kine musician. One of these guys. Which, I don' know, on account of white guys all look alike to me.

Dupree burst into laughter at this. Lyn reached across the table for the paper. She spread it out on her knees, Penn scraping his chair nearer to get a better look. It was another flyer for the Afterlife Carnival Choir. As before, they were wearing gorilla masks. Lyn grinned up at Dupree and Joel, sharing the lookalike joke. There was a string of venues and dates along the bottom. All of them in the recent past except the last. She whistled through her teeth, so skilfully Penn gazed at her in surprised admiration.

—Check this out, Penn, she said, passing him the flyer with her finger pointing to the last line of text.

—*King Kong Nite!* he read. *An All-Star Tribute to the Eighth*

Wonder of the World! Le Park Restaurant on Sunset Plaza. May 23, 8 'til late.

He looked around the table. That's tonight, Cicoira said, nodding his great head. Everybody was silent for a moment. The sound of a vacuum cleaner came from an upstairs window. Penn felt unaccountably pressured, like they were waiting for him to say something.

Lyn helped him out, asked Joel if he'd found the flyer in the boarded-up apartment. Joel nodded, Uh-huh, stack of the suckers. Music shit all over. She asked him if there'd been anything else there, maybe with the guy's name on. Joel said, Just a bunch a hippie shit, not like he'd sprayed his tag on the wall.

—If, said Penn, looking at Lyn over his tortoiseshells, it *is* a guy, of course.

—*Of* course, she said, not rising to the bait.

There was another silence. Penn did his jacket up, undid it. Usher looked at his watch, said, Well, you got a few hours to kill before you get to meet King Kong. Cad, I believe we may have some unfinished business? Wanna step inside, get a little closure on this?

Sitting in the cool of the book-lined study, Simon served them with tea and cookies (*biscuits*, he called them), white china on a silver tray. He didn't look at Penn at all, retreating wordlessly and softly closing the door. Neither Usher nor Penn had taken the chair at the desk. Usher poured the tea.

—An English thing, as much for Simon as me, he said. Don't like to upset his routine. Cookie?

Penn took the cup, rested it on his knee. He began to say something, anything, but Usher took over, speaking quietly and reasonably.

—There's this unresolved piece of business about the

house, he said. My son is mobilizing his lawyers on behalf of the estate. It's not going to be pretty, and, I have to say, I think they will find a way. Can you afford a lengthy court battle?

—Sure. If I sell the house.

Usher took a sip of his tea, placed the cup carefully on the desk, said, Well, I think I can see a way around this . . .

Through the window Penn could see Lyn walking with Joel in the garden. He knew this was the time, knew what he had to do, if she was ever to speak to him again. It's no big deal, he said. You can have your house back. I got it by a trick, whether you're happy with it or not. I hereby relinquish any claim on your property. I'll bring the paperwork and we can smoke it together. I'm afraid that I pretty much sucked your wall safe dry. Also, I'd like to keep the Harley and the E-Type, if you can find it in your heart.

Usher leaned back in his chair and laughed, slapping his bare knees. Cad, you continue to astonish me. I was about to suggest some kind of arrangement whereby you honored the terms of the estate and inheritance without giving the house back; a compromise. Are you serious about this? As you said, I'm happy. I have no problems with our arrangement, and no intention at all to renege on a deal. Why don't you think about it?

Penn turned his head to watch Lyn again, and smiled ruefully. I have thought about it, Ed, he said. Thinking like this is all new for me. I may get to like it. Nope, he said, getting to his feet and stretching, it never seemed like home to me anyway, to be honest, just a kind of dream. It's an undone deal.

—On one condition, said Usher. Before I accept, I want you to tell me what you want from life. I get the impression there's a lot of frustrated potential there, being misdirected at grabbing the side-effects. Let me explain? This place, Arkady, this was just a side-effect for me. I never set out to build a house. I set out to show people what I could do, what I was worth. Stand up and make a bit of noise, for the hell of it. This place just sort of happened. All this stuff, it's about *doing*, not having. So, Cad – Usher put a hand on Penn's shoulder – what do you want to do?

They stood by the window, watching Lyn by the pool. She'd just pushed Dupree into the water, bent double with laughter.

—Of course, said Usher, some things I can't help you with. The things you don't *need* help with.

Lyn was talking to Joel, watching Dupree wrestle the Harley upright in the water.

—Want to see something weird? Joel said.

—I'm up for that. Make a change.

He leaned over, hooking his lips apart with his fingers.

—Hng yuhknn ehrr . . . he said. Lyn took a wary peek into his mouth. Bright white smooth studs of new teeth pushing through his gums. A full set.

—Wow! she said. Joel snapped his lips back and chuckled.

—Weirdest thing, he said. Don' recollect ever having them babies before. Be on solid foods 'fore you can say gimme fries with that.

—It's the stuff like this happening to you guys that I just can't account for. Spiritual rebirth happens all the time, so they say. It's like shopping for groceries out here. But sprouting teeth, changing your body shape, losing tattoos, this is what makes the whole thing astonishing. Even for LA.

Penn strolled out and joined them, looking kind of strange. Lyn asked him if he was okay.

—Yeah, he said. For a homeless bum. Which is what I am. If you don't count the duplex.

—So you're really more just a bum, then, said Lyn, allowing her tone of voice to carry her real meaning.

Dupree called out to them from the pool, sitting astride the Harley, just his head above water.

—You guys wanna gimme some assistance here, we can wheel this sucker up the steps.

Penn looked at Lyn. But a bum with a bike, though, he said. Listen, I have a request. Want to hear it?

They walked into the shade of the loggia, Penn working on what he was going to say, and sat at the table where Simon had brought her tea about two hundred years ago. From the pool, splashing and laughter as Arthur and Joel jumped in to help Dupree with the Harley.

—Well? she said, smiling at him disconcertingly.

Penn pushed his hand back through his hair. *Well*, he said, it's kind of like this. You're the one round here been making all the calls over the last couple of days, right? I'm not saying you don't have the right, or that I'm not – Penn hunted for the word – *grateful*. Which I am, in a weird way. But I do have a request, and I'd like you to consider it.

Lyn laughed. You want me to jog around the block while you work up to it? You're not going down on one knee for this, I hope . . .

—More like coming in on one leg, I think. Okay. I know you're out here to do a job, and you're writing this stuff up as a newspaper story. I guess it's a pretty good story now, whichever angle you choose. So I understand it's important to you, and I trust you to do a fine job of reporting it and not make me out to look like an asshole. Assuming those two things aren't incompatible.

Lyn spoke through comically gritted teeth, moving her head from side to side. Enough preamble! Puh-*lease*!

—Okay! I'm sorry! Listen; don't write the story. Don't finish it. Rip it up. Please. I'm asking.

Lyn raised her eyebrows in surprise. Are you kidding? she said. This is the most important thing for me. It's what I do. It's my *job*. I really need this piece, and I've put in a whole lot of work on it.

Lyn was gesturing unthinkingly, with her hands now, suddenly animated. She stalled for a beat, searching the air for words.

—Penn, this is going to follow my last piece beautifully, everything's falling into place. This god-in-a-box thing is big enough on its own, but I've also found the guy that floated off into the sky, and he's playing in a band dressed as a gorilla. It's perfect. You can't ask me to drop it. You just can't.

Penn leaned forward in his chair, touched her knee briefly with his hand. Lyn, he said, I've never been so un-glib about anything in my life. You asked me why I'm really giving the box back, the reason underneath all the other good reasons. It's simple enough. I'm giving it back because you want me to. Because someone called Lyn Crowell, for whatever reasons, wants me to. That working over you gave me by the pool, when I was barely strong enough to stand, I saw something in your eyes. I saw something in there I never saw before. You want me to do it; okay. Don't get me wrong. I'm not doing it to please you, this is not an apple for the teacher. I'm doing it because it simply pleases me to do something you want me to. Call it more Cadogan Penn self-interest, if you like. And although I've given up a lot, mainly because you asked me to, I'm not calling in a favor here. You can have the moral high ground. I don't feel good up there; the air's too thin for me. I'm happier down in the smog with the animals. I'm not asking this for me, anyway. Believe it or not.

He waved his hand in the direction of the pool. It's for those guys. And Tischia. Your story, no matter how sympathetically written, will make them look like freaks. Once your story hits the streets, they'll get no peace from anybody. It's not fair. They may be angels or just human beings at their best, but they didn't ask for this to happen. I tricked them into this state, remember, like you told me. They shouldn't lose their right to individual privacy and anonymity if they want it. Which, apart from Shuggy, they clearly do. I don't want to bring ethics into this, I pull zero ratings in that department, but it does seem wrong to me to hang a lantern on these people. They have a *right* to be left alone. I understand that leaving them out of the story leaves you with no story. I understand that I'm asking you to make a sacrifice here. But I'm asking anyway. Please don't write the story. *Please.*

This gave Lyn a lot to think about. On the one hand, if she didn't write about the people who'd been affected by the box, it was just a shoebox. It was precisely the reality of the changes this bunch of individuals had exhibited that gave the story any content at all. On the other hand, she had given Penn a real mugging on moral grounds, him being just a thief and a con-man, and unfortunately he had her nailed on this one. If she submitted her story she was stealing something from these people; their right to be left alone. She'd be using them for her own ends. At root, it was her journalistic career that mattered to her, no matter how lofty she got about the Right of the People to Know the Truth, the noble calling of her profession. To her, this was just a story. To the guys who'd seen in the box, it was their lives. As she turned all this over in her head, shifting uncomfortably in her seat, unaware of Penn looking at her and trying hard not to smile too much, a way out began to emerge.

—What about Shuggy Kristiensen? she said. Hasn't he, um, let the cat out of the bag on this already? I'd just be putting a local incident like that into a wider context.

Penn gently patted the air with the palms of his hands. Shuggy, Shuggy, he said, shaking his head forlornly. Shuggy is just another publicity-hungry scamster in a town where those qualities aren't exactly at a premium. To the rest of the world, he's nobody in a bad suit. He'll get involved in his good works and the box thing will be forgotten. This was a classic Cuckoo Couch deal. People don't take it any more seriously than any other flake on the show.

—They took it seriously enough to blow up a poolroom.

—There are a lot of crazy people out there on a fuse shorter than Howard Stern's penis. Some guys' knee-jerk response to bed-head hair is to do a kindergarten drive-by. *The Shuggy Show*, this was entertainment. It was *television*. Next week it will be back to Elvis sightings. Really.

—Take a you pill on this?

—Take two. But avoid operating heavy machinery.

Lyn stretched back in the director's chair, turned her face up to the sun, sparkling through the vine leaves, her eyes closed.

—I guess, she said slowly, I could use the Shuggy incident as it was, as people saw it. That's like public domain, and it's not like he's scared of a little publicity. I need to see the guy, get it from his perspective. And if our box guy turns out to be who I think he is, I can get *his* story without involving our friends around the pool. Him, connected to the box on *The Shuggy Show*, there's a story there. Not the story I thought I was writing, which was going to net me a Pulitzer nomination, but I could do that.

—Sure, said Penn. You could do that as well.

She frowned at him. As well? As what?

Penn grinned. He loved it when he caught her out like this.

FIFTEEN

The Afterlife Carnival Choir Sings

Dupree and Joel climbed in the back of Lyn's Pinto.

—Niggers in the back of the bus! shouted Dupree as they pulled away from Arkady. Nothing changes nothing!

Penn unclipped his belt and fell clumsily between the front seats to the back, Lyn shouting at him to mind his goddam foot. He elbowed himself between Dupree and Joel, yelling, Niggers and trailer trash!

—You nuthin' but bone, Cadogan Penn, Dupree said, adding in a whisper, No wonder white women prefer us African-Americans in the sack.

Dupree started climbing over the passenger seat into the front, sitting on Penn's head momentarily. Lyn yelled at them all to behave, she couldn't see a damn thing, bunch of big kids climbing all over. Dupree settled in the passenger seat, buckled up. He started it, he whined, ludicrous popeyed expression on his face. Us negroes was fine till he started acting like he was one of the homies from the hood.

—I'm half black, retorted Penn from the back seat. Just not the skin part. Me and Michael Jackson, separated at birth. That guy's got a chest like a frozen pond compared to me. I love you black guys. And you love me. 'Cos I dig jazz. Kenny G. That piano guy, Phil Collins. Ain't that so, Joel?

—You the whitest nigger I ever see, said Joel. I wanna

197

grow up be jus' like you, shoot the hoops, hang out, drink paint.

—Teach me that handshake thingie you chaps do, Penn said, in his Prince Charles voice.

Joel looked at him and grinned, row of little white enamel buttons pushing through his gums. Ain't 'nuff time in the whole world, he said.

—Betcha I can do it before we get to Le Park, Penn said. By the time they got to Sunset Plaza it was ten before eight, and Penn's fingers were a bruised knot. Okay, okay, he said. I admit it. I am too white. Okay? I tried.

They'd erected a huge cutout of Kong over Le Park, with searchlights playing over it and sounds of roaring and gunfire coming from roof-mounted speakers, and there was a banner which read LE PARK HONORS THE EIGTH WONDER OF THE WORLD! Lyn slowed at the curb and the valet bent to her window.

—Good evening, ma'am. May I see your reservation?

Penn spoke up from the back. Reservation? We don't got no steenking reservation. What do you think we are, Indians?

—I'm sorry, sir, we're at capacity tonight. It's a phenomena. We just turned away the Chevy Chase party? Have a great evening, and thank you for the Sierra Madre reference.

The valet waved them on, Penn yelling, You can't even spell eighth! and a stretch limo took their place. Park around the corner there, said Penn. The people here know me, I'll get us in. I'll be right back.

Penn slipped out of the car and sidled around the corner, climbing over the white plastic chain and through the ferns up to the entrance.

—Steven! he said, pleased to recognize the face at the door. Steven moved him back into the ferns with his arm,

198

making way for a dark, Italian-looking guy with a crosseyed blonde on his arm.

—Mr George! he said, opening the door with a flourish. Fabulous you could be here with us tonight!

—We're delighted to be here, said Paul George in a deep, warm voice. Penn's mouth gaped open at his back as he went inside.

—Steven! The guy's a fucking panhandler! He passes out cards in the lot!

—Well, said Steven out the side of his mouth, smiling at another approaching couple, it's obviously a technique that works. Maybe you should try it. Excuse me.

Penn waited, dodged back in front of Steven. You gotta let us in, he hissed. It's important. Table for four, anywhere.

—In that case, we can put you out here on the sidewalk. Give me a break, Cad. I'm working. There's no room for four. I just turned away . . .

—Chevy Chase and his entourage, said Penn bitterly. Well, thanks for your help.

—And thank *you* for *yours*.

Penn slunk off through the shrubbery.

—We got ticketed just sitting here, said Lyn. Motor still running. Can they do that?

Penn leaned on the roof of the Pinto at Lyn's window.

—I got ticketed one time just for thinking about parking, said Penn. There was a sign saying don't even think of parking here and I *was* thinking about it. Look, I can't get us in. They're turning away B-list, and we're about Z. Any bright ideas?

Joel got out the car. Trouble with you guys, he said, you always makin' life too complicated. Follow the Wolverine. He crossed the street and went up to the side wall of Le

Park, a long blank stretch of concrete punctuated with strips of vine-hung trellis. Dupree, Penn and Lyn followed, looking at each other as if to say, why not? They joined him just as he swung open a strip of trellis, walked right on through the wall. *Whaaaa?* said Penn. They were in a low storeroom, dimly lit by the gap in a door off to their left.

—I'm not even going to think about what just happened, said Lyn.

Dupree chuckled. From the voices and footsteps right over their heads, Penn guessed they were under the mezzanine, just about exactly below where he'd buttonholed Cicoira and Usher.

—Okay, he said, what's the game plan here?

—Find the guy, said Dupree. Give him his box. This is not a superbowl play we're talking about.

—Find him before the band starts playing, said Lyn.

—Too late, said Penn, hearing the low thud of an electric bass. Come on, let's join the party. They stumbled to the door, emerging in the corridor to the kitchens.

—We don't look at all suspicious, do we? said Lyn. Dupree wearing full tennis whites, carrying the racquet, Joel in Wolverine garb, Penn carrying a metal suitcase, Lyn in daytime casuals.

—Are you kidding? said Penn. This is Hollywood. We're partying. Let's *mingle!*

Le Park was glowing with glass-shaded candles suspended from the ceiling, reflecting off the glasshouse roof. Every table was full, and the place buzzed with conversation and laughter. On stage, in front of an Empire State Building cutout with a stuffed gorilla hanging off it, four guys in monkey suits were getting behind their instruments. Penn's

200

entourage found an empty bit of wall to the side of the stage and liberated glasses of champagne from a passing tray. Penn shrunk back behind some hanging foliage as Steven skipped by and up the steps to the microphone.

—Ladies, gentlemen, simians, he said through a vicious feedback spike. He signaled to the sound guy up on the mezzanine, continued. Welcome to our own very special tribute to the eighth wonder of the world. Tonight, we have a special MC for this very special occasion. Put your paws together, please, for the king of the jungle, *Mis*-ter *Shug*-gy *Krist*-iensen!

Penn slapped his forehead. I do not fucking bel-*ieve* it! Taped soundtrack music blared from the speakers and the spot moved from Steven to play on the Kong display at the back. The gorilla swatted at a model plane on a string, clutched his heart, climbed down and staggered to the mike, where he pulled the gorilla mask off in a dramatic gesture. The lamps reflected off Shuggy's splendid bald skull. The crowd went wild, some guests going so far as to rise to their feet. Respect due, the guy's ratings made a rocket scientist sweat.

—Hello, and a big secret Shuggy handshake to all you hipsters and flipsters out in la-la land, he said, beaming broadly. I'm pleased to emcee this very special occasion because, as you know, part of the proceeds tonight will be going to the Gorillas Are People Too program, which sends our brightest stars into the darkest jungle to highlight the plight of our monkey cousins. We're honored to have Sigourney here tonight . . . Sigourney?

Penn was concentrating on the band. He bent to whisper in Lyn's ear, got distracted momentarily by the scent of her hair.

—I've narrowed it down to the guys with the guitars. I just remembered, there was a guitar in his apartment. I can't remember what it looked like, just that it wasn't black like that guy's bass. Or shiny like the set of drums. So it's one of those guys.

Shuggy introduced the band, skipped off the stage. The guys in the monkey suits launched into a reggae version of the oo-be-doo song from *The Jungle Book*. A few people took to the small dancefloor in front of the stage, amongst them Paul George and his crosseyed blonde. Penn made a sour face.

—Hey, said Dupree, slapping his hand on the strings of his tennis racquet, these guys are good.

—Wanna dance? asked Lyn.

—Sure! grinned Dupree.

They drained their champagne and gave Penn the glasses, moved out onto the floor. Joel watched Penn, how he was looking at Lyn.

—Pretty lady, he said.

Penn affected surprise. Oh? he said. Yeah, I guess so. He swallowed and looked around the room nonchalantly.

—Yeah, said Joel. An' she strong on you, caveboy. Tol' me.

Penn turned to Joel and grimaced. Yeah, *right*.

—Science. By the pool today. You inside with yo' man, me an' Lyn be vibin'.

The band had segued into the Kinks' 'Apeman'. Lyn swinging her hair round her head, Dupree miming guitar on his tennis racquet. Penn couldn't let this one drop. Really? he said with a light how-ridiculous laugh. Um, what did she say?

—Something 'bout you takin' her to Watts? Made no

sense to me. Says you try a number on her, show her how deep you are. Lyn get a real buzz outta that. Lady loves her man tryin' to impress. She *touched* by the deal. See through you like you was glass, no problem.

Penn felt like a fool. Shit.

—Hey! said Joel, digging him in the ribs. The fuck you sorry for? Want the lady to think you a asshole? Here she come.

Lyn's face was flushed and smiling. C'mon, Penn, do your moonwalk for me.

Dupree took the suitcase, pushed Penn onto the floor. The band was playing 'Monkey See, Monkey Do'. Penn essayed a few whiteboy steps, feeling totally out of place, hoping people weren't watching him. Lyn was grinning, her eyes flashing. The band was deafeningly loud out here.

—You're laughing at me, said Penn.

—What? said Lyn. Penn thought, what the fuck, and launched into a series of movements as extravagant as they were inappropriate to the beat. Any beat. Mercifully the band stopped and announced an interval. Shuggy came back into the spotlight just as the band were filing offstage.

—Come on! said Lyn, tugging Penn's sleeve. Dupree held out the case for him as they passed.

—Aren't you coming? said Penn.

Dupree glanced at Joel, shook his head. Your gig, he said.

Penn followed the band through the swing doors at the side of the stage, Lyn at his side. He still had no idea how to do this.

—Hey, excuse me? he shouted. The band paused, turned to look. A waiter pushed by with a tray of food. I have something for the guitarists in the band, Penn said, feeling more stupid with every syllable. The drummer monkey waved a paw at them and went into the dressing room. Not the bassist, said Penn. Another monkey disappeared. Penn looked at the guys in monkey suits. Wanna take your heads off there? he said. They did. One of them was black.

Penn coughed embarrassedly. Actually, he said, looking at the other guy, it's just for you. The black guy gave him an expression that said *enough* of this shit, and left them alone. All this had taken maybe eight seconds, and nobody had even stopped moving. The last remaining monkey had his hand on the dressing-room door. Older guy, maybe around fifty. He had a thin, clean-shaven face and long dark hair in a ponytail held with a green rubber band.

—What do you want? he said.

—You roomed off Tuscadero? asked Penn. Ground-floor apartment, suns all over the door?

—Sure. Why? What is this?

—This, said Penn, holding up the case. Your property. I'm returning it. I took it from your apartment.

—Could you tell us your name? Lyn interrupted. So we know we've got the right guy.

—Kent, he said.

Lyn looked disappointed. She'd been so sure, and now she wondered why. She passed Penn the key, and he unlocked the case and took out the shoebox. He stood and held it out to the guy with the ponytail, feeling that movement inside it, that swaying. He felt his fingers tighten around it. Could he really let it go? His hands shook.

—My *shoes*? said Kent, clearly mystified. You stole my *shoes*?

—No, no . . . began Penn, and suddenly, somehow, caught between the duty of giving and the instinct of taking, he fumbled the box, the movement in it unbalancing him.

The gift twine caught in his finger, slipped away. Kent went to catch it, flipped the lid . . . right off. Penn's heart jumped, and in an interval too short to measure he anticipated the blinding white light of god, thinking, This is it, I'm not ready, I'm not ready, oh *god* . . .

And a pair of shoes fell to the floor. Black Oxfords, lace-ups. Penn watched them tumble in slo-mo, bounce off the floor. Kent held the lid in one hand, the empty box in the other. Penn looked from the box to the shoes, dumbly, stupidly, unable to think.

—*Shoes*? he said, almost crying.

—What did you expect? said Kent. It's a shoebox. Hey, thanks and everything, but I never wear them. Keep 'em. Excuse me?

He went into the dressing room. Penn slid down the wall, sat heavily on the floor, weighing the shoes in his hands.

—I don't believe it, he groaned, shaking his head. I do *not* believe it.

—Well, Lyn said, looking at him slumped against the wall, maybe you never did.

Penn stared at the shoes. Was this *it*? He examined them minutely. Low-grade chrome leather uppers, composition sole showing a little wear. He squinted inside.

—Hell, they're not even my size.

Was he missing something? He grabbed the box. It was empty, no matter how hard he looked. He put the lid back on, felt for the movement. It wasn't there. Empty, he said, and tossed it aside.

Lyn knelt in front of him, touched his face. Have a little faith, she said. I never saw anything in it either. But I see something in you. You're not empty, Penn.

As he took hold of her hand, something inside him turned,

opened, woke up, and he began to smile; and the smile widened and broke into a laugh. A laugh that Lyn had not heard before.

—No, he said, I'm full of it. I'm *full* of it!

Filmography

I LOVE THIS TOWN!   Arkady Media Pictures
Prod. E. V. Usher. *Dir.* Cadogan Penn. *Screenplay* Lyn Crowell.
With Steven Park, Auburn Cord.

HAYRIDE IN HELL   Arkady Media Pictures
Prod. E. V. Usher. *Dir.* Cadogan Penn. *Screenplay* Lyn Crowell.
With Auburn Cord, Tyler Dupree.

TAKE A ME PILL, BABY   Pencro Productions
Prod. Cadogan Penn. *Dir.* Lyn Crowell. *Screenplay* Lyn Crowell.
With Nick Nolte, Tyler Dupree, Cadogan Penn.

Related Interest:

Tricia White:

Nazi Night Nurse, G-Spot Jamboree, Here's Hillary! The Story of a President's Wife, Thong of Norway, Skis of Desire, E-Womanuelle III, Homicide Love

The Tammi Trips:

Tarpit Derbettes the Movie, A Triangle Has Four Sides, King Leer, Jackoff's Three Sisters

Paul George:

Police Academy 15